"Somebody had it in for these two," Cliffie said.

About that, he wasn't wrong. I'd found two bodies in the woods, Neville and the Negro whose name, Cliffie assured me, was David Leeds. Neville had been shot in the face twice. Leeds had been shot in the neck.

"I just hate the idea of a colored man getting together with a white gal," Earle went on.

"Straight from the KKK handbook," I said.

Earle stomped away, angry.

"You better watch yourself around him," Cliffie said. "He doesn't like you much."

"I noticed that."

"But most people—a colored kid and a white girl— I don't like it myself."

The medical examiner came then. He wore his usual black topcoat, black fedora, black leather gloves. He carried a black leather medical bag, the type Jack the Ripper dragged around Whitechapel in the fog.

"How come you were out here tonight, McCain?"

"Neville was my client."

★

FOOLS RUSH IN

ED GORMAN

Linda L. Hubler
300 Spruce, St
FARMINGTON,
Minn
55024

WORLDWIDE®

TORONTO • NEW YORK • LONDON
AMSTERDAM • PARIS • SYDNEY • HAMBURG
STOCKHOLM • ATHENS • TOKYO • MILAN
MADRID • WARSAW • BUDAPEST • AUCKLAND

To Claiborne Hancock, of course

Recycling programs
for this product may
not exist in your area.

FOOLS RUSH IN

A Worldwide Mystery/January 2009

First published by Pegasus Books LLC.

ISBN-13: 978-0-373-26659-3
ISBN-10:   0-373-26659-6

Printed in U.S.A.

For many of those who suffer the incurable cancer called multiple myeloma, there was one person we turned to above all for information, guidance, and wit— Chris Hollyer. MM took your life, Chris, but it will never take the patient and gentle spirit you left behind.

PROLOGUE

I AM SITTING HERE waiting for social caseworker Jenny Kosek to finish testifying on behalf of my client Dink Holloway, the nickname stemming from the fact that he's about five-two and weighs just over one hundred pounds.

The May day is so warm and sky-blue that I want to get out of court and just run my red Ford ragtop up and down the old river road. It's like sitting in school on such a day and watching the minute hand on the wall clock piss you off by moving so slowly. Surely the nuns sneak in at night with screwdrivers and trick the timing mechanism in some way.

Of course, back in my school days I wasn't a lawyer and I wasn't accountable for the fate of an eighteen-year-old compulsive thief named Dink. Now I can't gaze out the window. I have to pay attention.

With this case Dink graduates from juvenile to adult court and I can tell you that the judge, who dealt with him when she worked juvie, is not happy to see him.

Jenny Kosek has clearly been seduced by Dink's charm. She doesn't even seem to mind that he is married and has at least one child somewhere among the local population. Quite an accomplishment for somebody of his callow years. He's a leading man in miniature, and the miniature gives him an advantage not even Charlton Heston and Rock Hudson have—most women want to (a) mother him and (b) put him on the path of the righteous.

Now, I'm as much given to a sociological view of criminality as anybody else in my time. Yes, poverty breeds crime; yes, it's difficult to escape the temptations of crime when your old man beats on your old lady and you have holes in your shoes; and yes! If only we combine patience with punishment, we will surely rehabilitate our criminals.

Even given my misgivings about Dink—I only took the case because his mother literally slapped my hands together and began, in between pleas, kissing them— Jenny's review of his history had me convinced that Dink deserved all the sociological pity and patience we could bestow on him. When Jenny described Dink's stealing the car only so he could take his dying grandmother back and forth to her medical appointments...well, as much as I'd laughed at him when he'd laid that particular myth on me—"You should be able to come up with a lot better stories than that by now, Dink! Shit, you've been stealing stuff since you were two!"—somehow there in the courtroom, and coming at the end of Jenny's longish retelling of the Dink story, somehow I felt kind of moved by it. Maybe the little prick wasn't as bad as he seemed.

And even the judge, Harriet "Hang'em" Hillman, dabbed once or twice at her eyes.

A month earlier there'd been some trouble in court, a man exploding when his brother testified against him. The man pounded his brother into unconsciousness before the guards at the back or the bailiff at the front could stop him.

Now, there was a cop in blue standing next to our table. He'd been glaring at Dink the whole day. As Jenny herself got choked up, the cop glowered at Dink again. He'd probably had to deal with too many Dinks in his time.

Jenny left the witness stand and the judge started to get up so she could go to her chambers and consider all she'd heard today. But then she stopped herself, sat back down, and said, "While I would ordinarily sentence you to time in prison—at least two years—I see a mitigating circumstance in the fact that you stole the car to help your grandmother. I condemn your lawlessness, but I applaud your humanity. I'm going to sentence you to five years of probation. You are to report to your probation officer twice a month. He or she will be assigned to you sometime in the next few days. Do you realize how fortunate you are not to be going to prison?"

We were standing up now.

"Yes, Judge," Dink said, sounding little-boy sincere as only he can. "I can't tell you how much I appreciate this. You've given me an opportunity to turn my life around completely."

Jenny choked on her tears so loudly, the effect was that of a gunshot.

All the usual followed: standing while the judge was leaving, interested people in the pews heading for the doors, the prosecutor coming over to shake my hand and tell me as always how much he liked my red ragtop, Jenny kissing me on the cheek and coming close to kissing Dink on the mouth, and the cop looking irritated that we were all standing around because he obviously wanted to get out of here and get back to shooting people.

So, finally, when it was all over and Dink and I were out in the hall and heading for the great outdoors, me thinking that maybe the judge was wise not putting Dink in the slammer—it was just then that the cop from the courtroom came exploding through the doors and said, "There you are, you little bastard!"

He didn't honor law or social rules. He just grabbed Dink by the hair, held him up a foot or two off the marble floor, and said, "Gimme back my billfold."

Dink looked at me with those spaniel eyes and said, "I didn't take his wallet, Mr. McCain. I really didn't!"

But the cop wasn't waiting. He jammed his right hand into the right pocket of Dink's lightweight jacket and pulled out a billfold.

"Oh, God, Officer! I don't have any idea how that got in there! I really don't."

Dink had, of course, picked the cop's back pocket. I was wondering what old Hang'em Harriet would have to say about giving Dink another chance now.

Don't worry. We'll see more of Dink later.

PART ONE

ONE

ON THE DRIVE OVER, I decided to leave it in the hands of the gods.

If Richie Neville's cabin door was unlocked, I'd go inside. If not, I'd turn right around in my red Ford ragtop and head back to my office. I wouldn't pick his lock, as I'd considered doing. State bars frown on lawyers who work night jobs as felons.

Neville lived just outside the city limits of Black River Falls, which, in this August of 1963, had reached 37,000 in population, thanks to an influx of young marrieds who looked upon us as a suburb equidistant from Cedar Rapids and Iowa City.

God had just flipped the switch and filled the early evening sky with stars. The stretch of river to my right was serving as a racetrack for speedboats, and on the far shore, among the moonglow birches, you could see campfires—hot dogs and s'mores and portable radios bursting with rock and roll—and in the ragged piney hills above, a freight train rattling through the prairie night.

Too good a night to risk my primary career as an attorney and my secondary career as a private investigator for the court of Judge Esme Anne Whitney.

But something ugly was going on, and it was that

very same Judge Whitney, who was also risking some serious legal trouble of her own, who'd convinced me that we both had to put a stop to it now.

For ten minutes I traveled a narrow gravel lane, and then I descended into a wooded hollow that smelled of loam and skunk and apple blossoms.

I pulled the ragtop off the road and stashed it behind a copse of hardwoods.

The rest of the trip would be on foot.

"YOU MEAN HER Negro boyfriend?"

"Yes, McCain, I mean her Negro boyfriend. His name is David Leeds."

We were in her courthouse office. This was about an hour before I left for the cabin. Thunder booming. Rain slashing the mullioned windows. And Her Honor, perched on the edge of her desk, shooting rubber bands at me and hitting me every other time or so.

She had a small box of the damned things on one side of her, and on the other side she had a snifter of brandy. Someday, years from now, when I was dying from a terminal illness and nothing mattered anymore, I'd find the courage to tell her about an organization called AA.

She tamped herself another smoke from her blue packet of Gauloise cigarettes. She was a good-looking woman in her early sixties. She escaped to New York whenever possible and that showed in the cut of the designer suits she favored and the faintly snotty way she dealt with plebeians such as me.

"Do a lot of people know about it?"

"They stay in Iowa City most of the time, thank God.

He's in school there. But it's bound to get around. That's the first problem."

"Well, she's what, twenty, twenty-one? It's sort of up to her, isn't it?"

"Why don't you just call me a bigot and get it over with?"

I smiled. "I was saving that for later, Judge."

"The fact is, I'm not a bigot at all. I merely want to see Senator Williams get reelected. And since he's a Republican, I'm sure you're more than happy about his daughter seeing a Negro."

She hooked another rubber band to her thumb and finger and let fly. It struck my small Irish nose and bounced off.

"I've never met Leeds. But I guess he's very bright. He's in law school, I understand."

"He's a Negro. A very handsome young man of twenty-one, I'm told, but a Negro nonetheless. And I say that with no prejudice whatsoever. You'll remember that it was my party, the Republicans, that freed the slaves."

"Oh, I already knew you weren't a bigot. You have a Negro gardener, a Negro horse groomer, and a Negro maid."

"I know you're being sarcastic, McCain, but that's just because your party didn't free the slaves."

There were several hundred arguments that came to mind but they'd be lost on her.

"So what we have," I said, "is a semipopular Republican senator in a tight reelection race this coming fall who doesn't want it known that his innocent young white daughter is dating a Negro."

She eased off the edge of her desk and walked over to one of the long windows, where she looked out at the wind-lashed summer trees. The rain tormented the glass. She held her elbow in the palm of her right hand and smoked with her left. I saw a watery portrait of her in the dark pane.

"You know what people see on television every night on the news, McCain. All these civil rights marches. All these threats those people make. Everything was fine a few years ago. I just don't know what happened. Anyway, most people are already stirred up by everything they see on the evening news. And if it were to be known that their beloved senator—and he is beloved no matter what you say, McCain—if they knew that the daughter of their beloved senator—a very beautiful young girl who has had every advantage a wealthy father could possibly have given her—if they knew that she threw everything away, including propriety and moral values…well, how could they ever vote for him?"

Now I got up, grabbed a bunch of her rubber bands, and walked over by the window. I began firing them at her from the side.

"So let me understand this, Judge. When you see all those impoverished people who haven't been able to vote or find decent jobs or send their kids to decent schools or do anything about all the police brutality generation after generation—it irritates you?"

She picked a rubber band from her hair and said, "Nobody has the right to break the law and march in the streets without a permit."

I couldn't keep the bitterness out of my laughter. "I'm glad you weren't one of Lincoln's advisers. He never would've gotten rid of slavery. And if you shoot one more rubber band at me, I'll start charging you a buck for every time you hit me."

She was mad and so was I. Most of the time our arguments had to do with her snobbery. She was, to her credit, able to rise above most of her prejudices in her courtroom. But when she wasn't in her judicial robes, she reverted to the coddled, cuddled old-money imperialist she usually was.

The arguments rarely got personal. This one was different. How could you see the shacks the marchers lived in, the degradation they had to put up with every day of their lives, and not in some way share their grief? How could you possibly watch the freedom marchers and not see how righteous they were in their simple but profound demands?

Who gave a shit about parade permits?

"But that isn't all, McCain."

"Oh?"

"Pick up the gray envelope on my desk."

I did so. There were photos inside of Lucy Williams and her boyfriend. Not dirty photos. If Lucy Williams and David Leeds had both been white or both been black, there'd have been no problem. Walking across the U of Iowa campus, his arm around her. Sitting on the same side of a restaurant booth. Her sitting on the handlebars while he was pedaling.

Innocent pictures. Two clean-cut, nice-looking young people in love.

"I see what you're talking about. Some people'll be offended by these, but they're really innocuous."

"These were sent to the party office in Des Moines.

Imagine if they made it into a newspaper." Then she said: "You once had a client named Richie Neville."

Maybe I was as slow as the judge frequently accused me of being. I didn't connect Neville to the photos until I remembered that he was a photographer now. When I'd represented him as a teenager he'd been nothing more than a harmless, garden-variety punk who'd gotten in juvie trouble in Chicago and had been shipped out here by his parents to live with his overly devout aunt.

"You're kind of jumping to conclusions, aren't you?"

"The senator's wife said she is sure she saw him two or three times driving past their house."

"How does she even know him?"

"He did yard work for them a few times. And now he's a photographer."

"Well, gosh, let's go lynch him then, since we've got such solid evidence against him."

"You're being ridiculous as usual, McCain. But I'll bet we could learn a lot by getting into his darkroom."

"You're ordering me to break the law?"

She had such a serene smile. "I'm not ordering you to do anything, McCain." The smile grew richer, deeper. "I'm just saying that if somebody were to be in the vicinity of Mr. Neville's cabin…"

THE RIVER SPARKLED in the moonlight. The rain had ended and all the foliage gleamed. Above me a raccoon was placing calls to other raccoons in a loud and endearing voice. The pines on both sides of the small, tidy cabin smelled sweet as a summer morning.

The raccoon was still jabbering as I surveyed the place. The exterior of the cabin was brown-painted sheets of plywood. A large window had been cut into the front of it, exposing the darkened interior.

Somebody, probably during one of Richie's notorious parties, had torn the door off the outhouse. Nobody was sitting in there reading *Playboy* in the dark.

Night birds and the sad solemn cry of an owl. The raccoon had fallen into a peeved silence. Screw them if they didn't want to answer back.

I wanted to make sure that nobody was around before I approached the door. It looked safe. I walked through the grassy space that served as yard. Before I touched anything, I slipped on the brown cotton gardening gloves I'd bought earlier at the A&P. Not for nothing was I a reader of hard-boiled paperbacks.

Despite the cool night breeze that carried the smell of pine, I felt myself sweating. Something was wrong here. I'd learned never to make assumptions, but I couldn't ignore the subconscious warning signals my body was sending me.

I reminded myself of my earlier decision. If the door was locked, I wouldn't go in. And I was assuming the door *would* be locked, what with all the expensive photography equipment inside.

I stabbed a finger at a piece of mid-level door and damned if the pine slab didn't swing inward.

The gods had decided.

Before going in, I played the light across the first few feet of scuffed and cracked linoleum inside. No evidence of blood.

I went in and played the beam across the destruction that somebody pretty angry had left behind. Neville's cabin was usually orderly. I'd done some legal work for him and he'd let me fish off his small pier. But the cabin was orderly no longer.

Neville's pride was his collection of blues records from the thirties and forties. Seventy-eight rpms and forty-fives, flung, broken, and smashed, lying across the debris that had once been a couch. A stuffed armchair, a nine-inch TV, as well as books, magazines, ashtrays, beer cans, Pepsi bottles, and smashed framed photos that had probably meant something to Neville littered the floor.

You always see rooms tossed on the silver screen. What you don't get is the violence of it, the jagged pieces of glass, the splintered thrusts of wood, and the stench of various liquids mixed together.

The beam revealed the chaos that extended from inside the front door to Neville's "church," as he called it. His darkroom. He was a local photographer of weddings, rodeos, and various civic and cultural events. People admired his work and he was always in demand.

I worked my leery way across the cabin, stumbling here, tripping there. The darkroom ran the length of the far wall. The door stood open.

The darkroom was more of a mess than the living area. An enlarger, a print washer, a print dryer, several lenses, a negative carrier, pans, and numerous other darkroom fixtures had been hurled to the floor. The chemical stench filled my nostrils.

Time to get out of here.

I'd just about worked my way across the rubble to the front door when car headlights swept across the front of the cabin.

Company had arrived.

THE SLIGHT MAN who emerged from the white Valiant sedan was maybe thirty. He was dressed in the kind of tight dark suit you saw in dance clubs where everybody did the twist—the slash pockets, the pegged pants, and the porkpie hat that the better grade of Chicago hood was wearing this year—and he was altogether as sleek as a stiletto.

But the shades were the startling part of his ensemble. Who the hell wore sunglasses out in the country at night? He leaned in through the open car window and doused his lights and cut off the engine. But he left the shades on.

I stayed inside, hiding. I wanted to see who he was and why he was here. This time when I took a quick look out the window, I saw he'd added one more piece to his outfit. A .45 that he'd just slid out of a shoulder holster.

This was Black River Falls, Iowa, where the worst violence we generally have is limited to high school kids getting into shoving matches after football games with fans of rival teams and engaging in that favorite working-class pastime, bar fights.

A gun?

I decided to step into the door frame rather than wait for him in here. Scare him less than if I was lurking inside the cabin.

I held up the badge I got as a court investigator. "I need you to identify yourself."

"Shit," he said.

He was turning and running back to his car before I was able to speak even one more syllable.

He ground the ignition key until the motor exploded

into life and then he backed up like a bullet, never turning the lights on. His tires found the gravel road and he fishtailed away with his porkpie hat, and the .45 I doubted he had the legal right to carry. I took my nickel notebook from my back pocket and wrote down the number of his Illinois plates.

I was walking to my car when I heard the whimpering in a wooded area west of the cabin. A dog. I remembered Neville's beautiful little border collie. Princess had one of those sweet faces that you want to carry in your wallet for emergencies. When the blues get bad, her face could help you get through.

The wooded patch was so dark I couldn't see anything resembling a path. I let her voice guide me into maybe three feet of undergrowth and then into the woods itself. A half dozen creatures crashed away from me in the bramble. Princess's whimpering never wavered.

The mournful sound of it scared me. I was afraid of what her voice was leading me to.

And it turned out my instinct was right. I had a damn good reason to be afraid.

TWO

"THIS MUST BE Lucy's boyfriend," Police Chief Cliffie Sykes said after arriving at Neville's cabin. "The Negro kid who was seeing Lucy Williams." He raised his flashlight high enough so that the edge of the beam washed across my face. "Or didn't you think I knew about that? I bet the judge and the senator sure didn't want that to get around."

It's hard to say which of us Cliffie hates worse, the judge or me. Probably Judge Whitney because he knows that she represents all he and his kin will never be—intelligent, reasonably open-minded, and eager to serve the greater good, the latter stemming not from virtue so much as simple patrician obligation. The best dukes always took care of the peasants.

This particular branch of the Whitney family fled New York due to a bank scandal created by the judge's grandfather. They came to what was little more than a hamlet and created the town of Black River Falls. They frequently took the train back to New York for a few weeks at a time. I imagine they needed respite from the yokels, my people. Various Whitneys served in all the meaningful town and county offices and ruled, for the most part, wisely and honestly.

But then the Sykes family made a fortune after

winning some government construction contracts. They were rich and dangerous. And they moved fast. Before anybody quite understood what was going on, the Sykeses had planted their own kin in most of the important political offices. Within two election cycles all that was left of the Whitney clan was the judge's office.

She hired me for a simple reason. She wanted to do her best to humiliate Cliffie. Whenever a major crime occurred, she put me on the case. After law school I'd gone back and taken night-school courses in criminology and police science, something, it is safe to say, that neither Cliffie nor his hapless staff had ever done.

We usually identified the culprit—bank robber, burglar, arsonist, and the occasional murderer—before Cliffie did. And thus the animus.

"Somebody had it in for these two," Cliffie said.

About that, he wasn't wrong. I'd found two bodies in the woods, Neville and the Negro whose name, Cliffie assured me, was David Leeds. Neville had been shot in the face twice. Leeds had been shot in the neck.

A voice from behind us said: "You think he was sleeping with her, Chief?"

The one and only Deputy Earle Whitmore, who said, on local radio, that if "those freedom marchers ever come up here," he wouldn't just use dogs and water hoses, he'd turn poison gas on them. Even for Cliffie that had been a bit much. Earle the Pearl had been forced to apologize to "the law-abidin' colored people of Black River Falls who know to not stir up no trouble lessen they get trouble right back." Probably not the apology Cliffie had in mind but it was better than the threat of poison gas.

"I just hate the idea of a colored man gettin' together with a white gal," Earle went on. "Makes me just want to go over to them bushes and puke my guts out."

"Straight from the KKK handbook," I said.

"Watch your mouth, Earle," Cliffie said, "or McCain here'll run and tell everybody what you said."

"Can't a man speak his mind?"

"Earle, goddammit, shut up—and I mean it."

A few months ago Cliffie, in an act of true bravery, had hauled two people from a burning car. He not only got written up admiringly by Stan at the paper, he'd even been interviewed on television. Even though most people still thought him incompetent as a police chief, they no longer laughed about him as a joke. The way he was treating Earle tonight indicated that he was enjoying his well-earned admiration.

"In fact, Earle, go back there and direct some of that traffic that's comin' in here all of a sudden."

Earle stomped away, angry.

"You better watch yourself around him," Cliffie said. "He don't like you much."

"I noticed that."

"But most people—a colored kid and a white girl— I don't like it myself."

The medical examiner came then. He wore his usual black topcoat, black fedora, black leather gloves. He carried a black leather medical bag, the type Jack the Ripper dragged around Whitechapel in the fog.

The TV crew had brought enough lights to illuminate a long stretch of woods. The light was almost as lurid as the corpses themselves, that too-harsh glare you see in crime lab photos.

"How come you were out here tonight, McCain?"

"Neville was my client."

"I suppose it's gonna be that attorney-client privilege thing."

"Afraid so."

"Did he know this Negro?"

"I don't have any idea. He never mentioned him, anyway."

"Judge know about this yet?"

"Not as far as I know. Haven't called her, anyway."

He nodded. "There's gonna be a lot of press on this. That's all you can see on the news these days. Negro this and Negro that. Personally, the government never did a damn thing for me, but if they want to live off the government, I guess that's up to them." Then: "I don't want you working on this case. I'm gonna find the killer and I'm gonna throw him in jail."

The New Cliff Sykes. He was now looking to score a double public relations coup. Pull two people from a burning car and then solve a racial murder.

"I can't promise you that."

"Well, then I can't promise you that I won't throw your ass in jail. There're a lot of laws against interfering with a police investigation."

"Yeah? Name one."

He spluttered. This was the old Cliffie, not the new, composed, beloved Cliffie. Well, beloved goes a wee bit too far, I guess.

"I don't pretend to be a lawyer. I never had the advantages you did."

Much as I didn't feel like laughing with two young men lying dead at my feet, I couldn't help it. "No offense, but your old man owns this town. He could've sent you to Harvard if he'd wanted to."

Then I laughed again for picturing Cliffie storming around the Harvard campus, picking fights wherever he went.

"I've given you fair warning, McCain. And I'm going to put it in writing, too. I'm going to write you a letter and I'm going to keep the carbon. So when I take you to court, I'll have the evidence."

Four reporters had just spied Cliffie and were hurrying over. Superman had nothing on our esteemed police chief. Clark Kent had to go into phone booths to change. Cliffie could swell up into the hero he'd recently become with virtually no effort at all. And he could do it standing in place.

One of the reporters said, "Do you think the March on Washington is going to inspire this kind of violence?"

Three days from now there was going to be a march on Washington, D.C., that the Kennedy administration was only reluctantly going along with. The national press was obsessed with it. Any local story that had any element of race in it was an excuse to bring it up. There was one hero in the land, at least for me: Dr. Martin Luther King. Despite J. Edgar Hoover's predictable warning that the march would be filled with "communists and agitators," Dr. King's hopes for the march buoyed everybody who believed that race had to be dealt with seriously for the first time since Reconstruction. The march was discussed on radio, TV, at picnics, family meals, church gatherings, fancy bars, blue-collar bars, everywhere. The topic was inescapable.

So of course, as the reporters gathered around him, Cliffie said, "Just what march on Washington are you boys talking about?"

The chest expanded. The campaign hat that was the same tan as the khaki uniform was tilted a more dramatic angle. And of course, his right hand dropped to the handle of his holstered handgun.

Slap leather, pardner.

As I walked back to my car, I heard one of the reporters say, "You mean you haven't heard about the March on Washington, Chief?"

The grounds were getting crowded. The gathering of ghouls had already begun. The triple features at the drive-in weren't that hot tonight, why not drive out and stand around a murder scene instead? True, nobody sold popcorn out here, but there was the chance you would get to glimpse a real true corpse. You wouldn't see nothing like that at no drive-in. No chance.

"YOU SURE YOU DON'T want no wine, Sam? It's the good stuff. That Mogen David."

Cy (for Cyrus) Langtry claimed he wasn't sure how old he was. He came up here with his grandmother, who had been a slave in Georgia before the war. He had spent most of his fifty years in Black River Falls as a janitor, first at city hall and later at the grade school. I imagined he was at least in his mid-seventies.

I went directly to his place from the cabin where the murders had taken place. He'd known David Leeds well. I wanted to be the one to tell him.

Anytime the temperature was above fifty-five you

saw Cy on the front porch of his one-story stucco house so close to the river that, as Cy liked to joke, he could probably fish out his back window if he wanted to.

At night he played records. His vision was so bad television was wasted on him. He'd sit on this throne-like rocker, in a white T-shirt, brown cardigan sweater, and gray work trousers. He usually wore sandals with no socks. He was now a shrunken little man with a raspy laugh and a thick pair of glasses that did him no good at all. I was never sure why he wore them. Next to him on the floor he kept his Mogen David and two glasses, the second one for any guest who might drop by.

When I pulled up, he was playing his favorite singer, Nat "King" Cole. Cy liked to tell the story of how back before the war he used to go to Moline, Illinois, some weekends to see Cole play when he'd make a midwestern swing of the better cafés.

I'd been around him all my life without ever really knowing him, until two years ago when the city tried to claim eminent domain and seize his property for some sort of warehouse. His daughter, who lived closer to town than Cy did, came to me and asked if I'd represent him for what she could afford to pay me. The way eminent domain is frequently used has always pissed me off. The rich get their way. I took it on for free, not because I was such a swell guy but because I didn't like the idea of kicking Cy out of the home where he'd lived with his wife and kids for so long.

Sarah, Cy's daughter, got to know David Leeds when he'd been going through her neighborhood one day looking for yard work. She'd taken him out to Cy's place a few times. David loved listening to Cy's stories. And, as Sarah said, he didn't seem to mind the free wine, either. Cy always kidded David about all the jobs he did to support his college habit. Yard work, car-washing on Saturdays, farm work when he could get it, and employment as a dance instructor a few nights a week. That was the one Cy couldn't get over. But David was a good-looking kid, he had that big-city patina about him, and he worked for a studio that taught all the dances on *American Bandstand,* while ballroom dancing and the like were left to Arthur Murray.

The plan was for David to sleep on Cy's couch all summer. There was a big detasseling operation that worked out of town here. Detasseling paid better than even factory jobs and you damned well earned it. I de-tasseled for two summers and I rarely had dates. Too tired even on the weekends I didn't work.

"You sound kinda funny tonight, Sam."

"Guess I'll have some of that wine."

"Help yourself."

I did, downing half a glass of it in a single gulp. Bombs away.

Crickets and river splashing on rocks and lonesome half-moon and the sound of distant ghost trains.

I spent a minute or so trying to figure out how to tell Cy about it, and then I just said, "Somebody murdered David tonight, Cy."

I don't know how I expected him to react. He rocked back and forth. He said nothing, then "Figured it'd be something like that, the way you sounded, so funny and all."

"I'm sorry. I'm going to find them."

"You sound like Marshal Dillon on *Gunsmoke*."

"I'm not tough, Cy. You know that. But I can get things done when I need to."

"Whites killed him."

"Probably."

"Bastards."

I had never heard him use language like that. It shocked me because it came from him and then saddened me because I heard the tears that overcame the rage in those words.

"Bastards." A lifetime of anger, frustration, humiliation, fear, and ruined hopes in that single word.

The night birds had never sounded more mordant as we sat in the terrible echoes of that single word, of all the sorrow in that single word.

"He wasn't perfect. Drank too much. Ran around with white girls too much. He even tole me one night we was helping ourselves to the jug here about how he pulled off a couple robberies back in Chicago. But that don't give no white bastard the right to kill him."

"It sure doesn't."

"And anyways, he tole me that when a friend of his got sent up, he quit doin' bad stuff and buckled down and got himself a partial scholarship." Clink of bottle neck on glass. This time he didn't offer me any. He sat back and started rocking in his chair. "I think he knew something was comin'."

"I'm not sure what you mean."

"That white girl, Lucy. He said she was all tensed up lately. So many people on them. Her folks and that rich boy she used to go out with. And then them bikers always following him around and makin' fun of him.

She told him she had nightmares about something terrible happenin' to him."

"How did *he* feel about it all?"

"Oh, it was getting to him, too. Reason he always liked our town here was because folks were nice to him. He said he never seen so many nice white folks. The bikers and them like that, they didn't like him. But I mean most folks—we got a nice little town here, Sam. Still is. Even when he was goin' out with Lucy, people still hired him for the jobs he did. And was nice to him and everything. But there's always a few—"

I stood up.

"I'll find them, Cy, the ones who did it."

"There you go soundin' like Marshal Dillon again." He'd allowed himself the one joke. Then: "The colored, we've had to put up with shit like this all our lives. I want you to get 'em, Sam, and get 'em good and don't let that stupid bastard Cliffie get in your way, either."

Rage and tears, rage and tears. Job was the only book of the Bible that held any meaning for me. Rage and tears against the unfathomable ways of God. Or as Graham Greene put it, "the terrible wisdom of God." If there was a God. And if not, rage and tears against the unfathomable randomness of it all.

"You do me a favor and go in there and turn up Nat for me?"

"Sure."

Cole was singing "Lost April," one of my favorite songs of his. The wan melancholy of it matched my mood exactly.

THREE

"You know, Mr. C, you should write a book about all your experiences. Look at Sherlock Holmes. He wrote a lot of books."

In case you haven't met her before, Jamie is my secretary. She was free when she was part time, now she was full time and I paid her.

I'd represented her father in a property-line case and he ceded her to me as a form of payment. We don't discuss the fact that she was nineteen when she graduated high school—she once vaguely alluded to the fact that she had to take eleventh grade over again because she couldn't remember the lyrics to the school fight song—nor do we mention the fact that if murder was ever declared legal the first person I'd shoot was her boyfriend, Turk, who combines the most annoying mannerisms of Marlon Brando and James Dean and that New Zealand tribe said to wash themselves only once every full moon because they fear water will eat their flesh.

Judging by the responses of my male clients, Jamie will never have to want for men eager to woo her. She's one of those women blessed with a face and body that will keep her looking like jailbait until she's well into her thirties. The fact that she can only type sixteen words a minute, and not all of them exactly what you would call words, and that she frequently forgets to write down phone messages—they are as nothing compared to the luxurious promise of that body and the merry gleam of those blue eyes.

"He isn't still alive, is he?"

I'd been studying a brief I needed in court this morning and had been trying hard not to pay attention to her usual babble. My terrible secret is that I have my own fantasies about Jamie—how could I not?—and I even like her because for all of her mindless prattle, there is a genuine sweetness in her that's rare in our species. She's a good, if daft, kid. And it doesn't hurt that, as demonstrated this morning, she's picked up on the see-through-blouse trend.

"Sorry, Jamie. What did you say?"

"Sherlock Holmes, Mr. C."

The "Mr. C," by the way, comes from the Perry Como TV show. All of Perry's regulars call him Mr. C. Jamie thinks this is pretty cool. That my name starts with "Mc" doesn't deter her in the least.

"Sherlock Holmes?"

"Yes. I was saying he wrote all those books and you should, too. You know, about your experiences."

"Ah. I see."

"Like what happened last night out at that cabin. That would make a chapter in itself."

"Yeah, but I sure couldn't write like Sherlock."

"Is he still alive, by the way?"

The phone, in its mercy, rang.

"Well, you made the wire services this morning," Stan Green said. "AP and UPI both. Do I get an exclusive if I buy you lunch?" Stan is the *Clarion*'s managing editor and one of its three reporters.

"That would depend on whether you can take a late lunch and if you're willing to spend at least sixty-five cents for my food. That would mean ham, lettuce, mayo on white bread with the crusts cut off and a small fountain Coke at Woolworth's."

"You are one crafty bastard, McCain. One-ish?"

"One-ish will do it."

"God, I hate politicians." A phone rang behind him. "Gotta go."

"Turk wants to write a book," Jamie said after I hung up.

I looked at her. She's one of those girls who wears ponytails well. I just smiled at her for making me feel good for at least these few moments. She really is sweet.

"Of course," she said, "I'd end up doing most of the writing."

I was still within the wonderful beatific moment she'd inspired with her odd innocence and her jutting blouse. Jamie and Turk writing a book together? Of course. All things were possible in my beatific if transient world.

THE MOST VALUED ITEM in Woolworth's wasn't anything on sale. It was a booth in the luncheonette. There were five of them. The rumor was that you had to get up before dawn and stand at the Woolworth's front door until they opened. Then you had to leap over entire aisles of merchandise and catapult into a booth, which you had to occupy for hours before the lunch menu was available.

So it surprised me that Stan was sitting in a booth. He wasn't alone.

The girls in my high school class used to play an interesting game called One Word. You were given one word to describe a person. If the game was played with beer present, it quickly degenerated into stupidity. "Fat." "Icky." "Smelly." Anything that would get a giggle.

But if it was played sober, it revealed interesting and sometimes serious perceptions of people you knew.

The word for Stan was "slovenly." When he'd first come to town ten years ago, he'd been a dude. It was rumored he even swam at the Y in one of those three-piece suits of his. But then his wife left him for an old flame, moved to Denver, and left Stan bereft of hair (he got bald within six months of her leaving) and even more bereft of grooming. He had two suits. He wore one till it got stiff with sweat and various other goodies and then put on the other one. His ties must certainly violate some civil code somewhere, given the fact that they look like an artist's palette. Except that the colors are stains of various kinds. The spaghetti and the mustard stains are the easiest to guess. The others are more obscure. His only known vice is bowling. As a vet, he spends most of his time at the Legion Lanes, where, upon occasion, he has been known to take home one of the bowling gals. He has a round, good-natured face that gets sort of wan whenever the subject of his wife comes up. She has yet to divorce him. She may just be test-driving this rodeo guy. We're all afraid that she'll come back to him someday. Nobody doubts that he'd build her a mansion if she did.

I could only see the back of the woman Stan was talking to.

I walked over to Stan and slid in next to him.

"Sam, this is Marie Leeds. She's David Leeds's sister."

Marie Leeds possessed one of those faces so regular of feature you wanted to study it. Not great beauty, this face, but certainly pretty. She nodded. "I came out here from Chicago two days ago to spend some time with David."

"I'm sorry about your brother."

"If I start talking about him, I'll cry. What I'd prefer to talk about is how serious this investigation is going to be."

"She talked to the chief of police," Stan said, "and said that he was very polite and friendly but she sensed that he might be a little—"

Marie's smile surprised me. It was a little girl's smile and it was a treasure. "'Stupid' was the word I used."

Her smile relaxed me and I sensed it had done the same for Stan. We were no longer representatives of the white race and she was no longer a representative of the Negro race. Not that we were such great grand friends but we were at least just human beings talking to each other.

"All the information he gave me came from the newspaper on his desk. Turns out Stan wrote it. Doesn't the chief file reports?"

"Well, in his own way he does. He used to have a very bright deputy who did most of the work in that area. But then the deputy couldn't take it anymore and got a job in Cedar Rapids."

"That deputy he has now—that Earle?—he just sat there with his arms folded the whole time I was talking to the chief. The only thing he said was, 'This is a small town and your brother acted like it was a big town.' A font of wisdom." She looked directly at me. "By that I take it Earle meant that David was seeing a white girl."

"That's what we've been told," I said.

Marie shook her head. "An ambitious young man like my brother, his good looks caused him a lot of trouble. He always said he preferred to live the way white people did. If you saw a job opening, no matter what it was, and you thought you could do it, go up and apply for it. And if you saw a girl you wanted to date, go up and ask her." She looked at Stan now. "Not that he made a big thing out of dating white girls. Most of his girlfriends were Negro. But every once in a while he'd get serious about a white girl for a while—he always taught dance lessons because it was easy money and he sure met a lot of young women." The wonderful girly smile again. "David was never much for staying with one girl long, whatever their color was. He liked variety."

"Marie raised him," Stan said. "Her folks were killed in a fire."

"You don't look much older than he was," I said.

"Seven years older. They died when I was seventeen." This smile lacked the energy of the others. "Here I said I didn't want to talk about him and that's all I *have* been talking about."

Discreet tears filled the corners of her eyes. She dabbed at them with a piece of tissue.

"I really don't want to be emotional about this. I want to find out who killed him. And emotional won't help me get there." Another dab at her eyes. "I teach seventh grade and that's what I try to teach my students. Anger, especially righteous anger, can get people up on their feet. But to get things done, you have to hold a tight rein on your feelings."

"I'm afraid you're right," I said.

"That's why I admire Dr. King," Marie said. "He's exactly the sort of person I'm talking about."

The waitress came, took our order, and fled back to the counter to call it in. She was frantic. By this time the lunch area was jammed. Some customers had to stand behind the stools to eat their lunch.

I'd just picked up my cup of coffee when the frantic waitress returned and said, "Are you Sam McCain?"

I nodded.

"There's a call for you. There's a phone at the far west end of the counter."

I knew who was calling and I knew why she was calling and I knew why I was mad she was calling.

"Just do me a favor and tell her I'm not here."

"Really?" the waitress said.

"Yeah, really. And I appreciate you doing it for me." She hurried away.

"The judge?" Stan said.

"Who else?"

"You have a very strange relationship with her. Really passive-aggressive."

I glanced at Marie and laughed. "In case you couldn't guess, Stan's minor at Northwestern was psychology."

Marie blessed me with one of her sweet smiles again.

FOUR

THE COLONIAL-STYLE house gleamed pure white in the early afternoon sun. Ellen Williams, the senator's wife, was tending to her garden of roses as I pulled up the drive.

Karen Porter, not only her friend but her partner in their downtown flower shop, was watering plants further downhill. She gave me a big wave and a big smile. I'd always felt much more comfortable with her than with Ellen.

Ellen turned when she heard my engine. She just stared at me. I'd never had the feeling she cared much for me, but because I worked with her good friend the judge, she was always polite.

While the house wasn't a mansion, it had a mansion's sprawl, grass so green it looked slightly unreal stretching east to a forest and west to a plateau, where an enormous white gazebo sat twenty yards from a tennis court and covered swimming pool.

Lucy Williams sat in the gazebo with her friend Nancy Adams. Even though Lucy was talking, there was an Andrew Wyeth loneliness in the juxtaposition of the frail blonde girl in the tennis outfit and the forlorn air she radiated even from here.

I parked and walked over to Ellen.

"Hello, Sam," Ellen said, striving to put some warmth in her voice for me. "Esme called and asked you to call her if you stopped by."

Ah, yes. Esme. Wasn't that French for relentless?

"I'll give her a call when I finish here. I'm sure she explained that she's asked me to look into this whole thing with David Leeds."

She was one of those erotically overweight women, the type favored by the Brits at various times in their bloody history. The face was what did it, that sensual mouth more than anything. Even in a pair of slightly baggy yellow walking shorts and a yellow sleeveless blouse, there was a sexual dynamic. I wondered if she was even aware of it. I wondered that especially now when the blue eyes held a quality of fear.

"I wish Lucy had listened to us." The trowel in her hand pointed upward like a dagger. The gloved hand seemed to tighten on the handle. "We begged her and begged her." The face tightened, while the dyed red hair blew in the breeze. "She owed it to her father not to get involved. His career is everything to him. He's the third senator in the family."

Five generations of Williamses, three senators. By now we were talking divine right. The bitterness in her voice let me know that her husband's career was everything to her as well. Her daughter didn't seem to be much more than an encumbrance.

"All right if I talk to her?"

"Personally, I wish you wouldn't. But Esme says it's important, so I suppose you should."

"I won't keep her long."

"You can keep her forever for all I care. My poor husband. I've never seen him like this. The election was close enough. Now, with this—"

Just then a red MG appeared in the drive. Two young men in tennis whites. Rob Anderson, Lucy's former boyfriend. Nick Hannity, a noted college football player.

When she saw them, she said, "You know, Rob would forgive her in a minute."

"For what?"

"For—seeing a colored boy."

"Oh."

"You don't seem impressed. But I am."

"Were they going out when she started seeing Leeds?"

"No—she'd already broken it off. She thought Rob was getting too possessive and she wasn't ready to be married to him. They were supposed to be married this summer, you know." She watched as the two young men in whites strutted toward us. "He'd still marry her, that's what I meant about his forgiving nature. He'd forgive her and still marry her."

"I think I'll go down to the gazebo." The way she talked about Anderson, he sounded like a master on a plantation. He would forgive her even though they hadn't been going out at the time she was seeing David Leeds. How big of him.

I was never eager to talk to Rob Anderson or anybody like him. His father was a very successful businessman who walked the dark side of the street, running loan companies that exploited the poor. He'd once made a martini crack about Judge Whitney that had pissed me off unduly. I managed to tromp, with great fervor, on his tennis-shoed foot as I left the party. He knew I'd done it on purpose but he could hardly say that without sounding paranoid, now could he? Especially after I'd made such a show of apologizing.

I think Lucy sensed me rather than saw me as I made my way down the hill to the gazebo. She lighted her new cigarette with her previous one.

She still hadn't looked at me when I stepped up on the gazebo. "Hi, Lucy. Your mother said I could talk to you."

"My mother says a lot of things, Mr. McCain."

Impossibly young, impossibly pretty, impossibly tortured, as you could see with a glance at those enormous brown eyes. The whispered word was that she seemed even more troubled following her stay in a mental hospital. They'd been trying to break her away from David Leeds. It hadn't worked. Most folks seemed to feel sorry for her parents but not for her.

Nancy Adams, a very pretty slender brunette also in tennis whites, said, "I'm going for a little walk."

"You don't have to," I said.

"It's all right, Mr. McCain."

"I'm supposed to play tennis," Lucy said after Nancy went over to talk to Karen Porter.

Lucy sat, prim and sort of casually regal, on the bench that ran around the interior of the gazebo. Her blonde hair was stylishly wind-mussed and the sorrow-shaped mouth had never looked more kissable than now in her deepest grief. Her long, tanned legs were wonderful.

She looked up at me and said, "I always thought you

were kind of nice, Mr. McCain. I'm disappointed you agreed to help them. I suppose it's because of Esme."

"People are just trying to figure out what happened, Lucy. Two young men are dead."

"Some bigot killed them. Have you seen what's going on in the South? It's on TV every night. Something like that happened to them."

"You mean they were killed because David Leeds was a Negro?"

"Yes. Exactly."

"But then why would they have killed Neville? He was white."

"Because they were friends. Good friends."

Judge Whitney had told me that Neville might have been the one to send photos of David and Lucy to the party office in Des Moines. Good friends?

But I didn't get to finish up my questions because Rob and Hannity were here. Rob was the sinewy type with a kind of mild contempt on his handsome face. He seemed to believe that God had put the rest of us here for his amusement. He walked over to Lucy and said, "If you want a lawyer, Lucy, let me get you a real one."

"Sorry to hear you flunked out of law school, Rob," I said. "Not even Daddy could save you this time, huh?"

He didn't lunge at me. Hannity, good watchdog that he was, did. But Lucy was already on her feet. "For God's sake. David's dead and you're all acting like brats."

We all froze in place at her words. I heard Rob say to himself, "David." Scornfully.

"I'll talk to you later, Lucy," I said.

Hannity was still glowering at me. He'd beaten up

the son of a client of mine. We'd pressed charges. He got probation. He didn't like me much and I liked him even less. Predators are bad enough. Predators born with silver spoons up their asses are even worse.

"Why the hell would you want to talk to somebody like him?" Rob Anderson said, making sure I heard him.

"Just shut up, Rob. I told you on the phone I didn't want to play tennis anyway. David's dead. You don't seem to understand that."

Ellen Williams was gone when I reached the house. I took a last look at the gazebo. Hannity was still glaring at me.

Then Ellen was coming quickly down the steps from the screened-in back porch.

"There's some news, Sam. Wait for me!"

I couldn't read her excitement. Was the news good or bad? She put her hand on my arm and said, "Esme just called. Sykes just arrested one of those horrible motorcycle hoodlums for killing Neville and Leeds." She gripped my arm even tighter as her face broke into a smile. "This should help, an arrest this soon. The focus will be on the killer and maybe not on Lucy so much."

"Just remember Cliffie's track record," I said. "He usually arrests the wrong person."

The eyes reflected instant anger. "Esme tells me that you're a wiseacre and now I can see that for myself. My husband's career is on the line here and I give you some good news and you do everything you can to knock it down." She nodded down to the gazebo. "I'm going to speak to Esme and tell her that I don't want you around my daughter at all. If she needs a lawyer, we'll get my uncle. Now, good-bye."

Only when she turned and walked back to the porch did I notice that all three people in the gazebo were watching me. I wondered if they'd been able to hear what Ellen had said. The way Anderson and Hannity were smiling, I assumed they'd heard every word.

Karen Porter, my one friend here, waved good-bye to me, smiling as always.

OUR TOWN LIKES to claim that its jail once held Jesse James, well-known psychopath and shooter of unarmed people, for a few days back in the bloody prime of the James-Dalton gang. While it's true that the James boys favored Iowa as a hiding place, they did most of their hiding just inside the Iowa-Missouri border. The man we got, close as we could figure, was a man named Niles Wick, who was a gang straggler.

Of course, in my growing-up years, none of us kids accepted the Niles Wick story. We preferred to believe that the name was simply one Jesse used. In those days, our jail was located one block east of the Royale Theater, the best second-run movie house anywhere, so we could load up on popcorn and a couple of flicks about Jesse—in these Jesse was a persecuted saint of course—and then we could run to the jail and stand on the corner and imagine Jesse looking down at us from behind the bars on the second floor. He looked like either Tyrone Power or Roy Rogers, take your pick. Both men had essayed him in film.

There was a new jail now, and it was located on the third floor of the recently built county courthouse. The design was severely functional, the material was a step up from cinder block, and the overall look was so dreary that you felt the prisoners could be sprung on a charge of cruel and unusual just for having to stay inside.

Cliffie's uncle, a man named Merle who had formerly been an auctioneer, laid out the plans and used his own construction company to build this monument to civic corruption.

There were at least a dozen Harley motorcycles in the parking lot. Ellen had been right. A biker had been arrested for the murders.

Inside, I said hello to Cliffie's sister, the receptionist; and the same to Paul the elevator operator, Cliffie's second cousin; and finally to Norman, Cliffie's first cousin and the front-desk day man at the police station on the third floor.

"No call for you to be here, Sam," Norman said, pushing his thick glasses back up his short nose. "My cousin's got everything under control. Case is all wrapped up."

"I was just wondering if the accused man has a lawyer yet?"

"He's guilty, Sam. Why would he need a lawyer?"

"You mean he's confessed?"

Norman grinned with gray teeth. "He will, time my cousin gets done with him."

"MISCEG—. DAMN, I can never say that word."

"Miscegenation."

"Yeah, that's the hot one now. Forbidden love. Black men and white women. Misceg—"

"No black women and white men?"

"No sizzle."

"'Sizzle'?"

"That's the word my editor always uses. 'Sizzle.'"

In case you're wondering, the writer I was talking to was not F. Scott Fitzgerald or Ernest Hemingway.

The writer I was talking to was Kenny Thibodeau, the official pornographer of Black River Falls, and not least of all, my best friend since we made our First Communion together nearly twenty years earlier.

On a trip to San Francisco four years ago, where he hoped to set eyes upon his idols Jack Kerouac and Allen Ginsberg, Kenny read some of his poetry one night at a coffeehouse. Believe me, Kenny is to poetry what I am to astronomy—nowhere.

But this guy came up afterward and said, "I really like your poetry." I'm sure that Kenny was secretly as shocked as I was when he told me the story. Even he knows his poetry stinks.

But the guy wasn't finished. "You ever thought of writing novels?"

"Sure. Who hasn't?"

"How'd you like to make four hundred dollars for a novel?"

"Are you kidding?"

"No, I'm not. You ever hear of the Midnight Secrets line of books?"

"The ones they keep under the counter in cigar stores and like that?"

"Yeah, in hick burgs they keep them under the counter. Where you from by the way?"

"Iowa."

"Iowa. I went through there during the war. You've got some nice-lookin' broads back there."

Kenny didn't mention that almost none of those nice-looking broads would have much to do with him. Or me. We had yet to grow into the charming, witty Cary Grant-like figures of our later years.

"You know how they work, don't you?"

"'How they work'?"

"No dirty words. No explicit descriptions. We generally like it when breasts are compared to fruit and when orgasms are compared to tidal waves. The thing is to make them *think* the stuff is really dirty. But we know better, don't we, Kenny?"

"We do?"

"Sure. Because if it was really dirty we'd all be in prison."

"I guess that's something to keep in mind. Prison."

"So anyway, Kenny, tell you what. You walk out to my car with me and I'll just give you copies of our two latest books, *Pagan Pussycats* and *Niagara Nymphos*. You take them and read them and before you leave town you give me an outline and three chapters. If I like what I see, I give you a hundred fifty on the spot and you go back to Iowa and write the rest of the book. How do you like the sound of that, kid?"

"Can I still write my poetry?"

"Kid, you can write all the poetry you want as long as you meet our deadline."

"How much time will I have before I turn my book in?"

"Three weeks."

And thus was born, among many other Kenny Thibodeau pseudonyms, Brace Bryant, Cal Cavalier, and Jack Hoffman.

But those were the days of jocularity when you could smirk at the ridiculous business Kenny was in, exploiting serious topics such as civil rights to idiotic ones such as how many stewardesses you could shove into the arms of a studly airline pilot.

But today neither of us was in a joking mood. Kenny said, "I'm thinking of driving down to Birmingham with my .45. Wanna ride along? You see that TV special last night?"

"Yeah. I'd like to kick Bull Connor around for three or four hours and then set him on fire."

"Right after I get done whipping him, man."

"Son of a bitch. I had to turn the set off. I couldn't take it."

Eugene "Bull" Connor was the Birmingham, Alabama, commissioner of public safety who had turned not only fire hoses but dogs on civil rights demonstrators. It was hard to watch the barrage of water and brutal cops pounding, kicking, and stomping people. And then he'd added those dogs.

The problem was that it was all being laid on Southerners. We lived close enough to the Missouri border to know that not all folks of the Southern persuasion were anything like Bull baby or his henchmen. And discrimination and violence were hardly limited to the South. Try walking down the street hand in hand with a Negro girl in Cicero, Illinois, sometime, or in parts of Chicago or border towns in my state. Or a hundred other northern towns.

Kenny said, "You think the biker killed that Leeds kid?"

"Too early to know."

"I wouldn't doubt it. Couple of them beat up those two Negroes at the county fair last year."

"Yeah, and got a weekend in jail for it."

"Surprised Cliffie went even that far."

We sat on the front steps of my office. A sleepy burg; a sleepy, hot afternoon. Turk had called and decided to break up with poor Jamie again—this generally happened once a week—and since neither Kenny nor I could take her sobbing, we sat out here with Pepsis and Lucky Strikes, just like the high school kids at least a part of us would always be.

"What's funny is that Lucy's old man seems to think nobody knew she was seeing Leeds."

I'd told him what the judge had told me. Kenny knows most of the worst people in town, so he helps me investigate sometimes by seeing what's going on in the Black River Falls underworld, if there is such a thing.

"So a lot of people knew?"

"Not a lot. But you know how gossip gets around."

"Then the senator is way behind if he thinks he can keep his daughter out of this."

Kenny, with his little tuft of chin beard, his long dark hair, and his dentist-deprived teeth, still and forever an honorary citizen of City Lights Bookstore in old San Fran, said, "Hell, I want him to lose anyway."

"So do I. He's a robber baron. But I hate to see Lucy dragged through this. And all the people who're gonna put her down."

"It's gonna be a bitch."

Jamie, bless her, still sniffling, came to the door and said: "It's the judge. She sounds really mad." She instantly began bawling again.

"Catch you later," Kenny said.

"Ask around, see if you hear anything."

He grinned. "Philip Marlowe is on the job."

I followed the sobbing Jamie inside, lifted the receiver from where it rested next to the phone. "Hello?"

"How professional of you to have a weeping girl answer your phone."

"I was going to call you first chance I got."

"I'm too angry to even talk about how you've been avoiding my calls all day. We'll deal with that later. Right now I need you to get out to Reston Park at the big pavilion."

"A picnic?"

"Lucy Williams called me. She said I wasn't to tell her parents about this. She wants to talk to you right away. Now get out there."

She slammed her receiver down.

"Do you think Turk and I'll get back together, Mr. C?"

I went over and put what I hoped was a brotherly arm around her and kissed her tear-warm cheek. "Sweetheart, you go through this every week. Of course you'll get back together."

She looked up at me with those guileless eyes and said, "Really?"

"Really."

"Oh, thank you, Mr. C. Now I feel a whole lot better. Thank you so much."

I was going to ask her not to be sobbing when she took the next phone call but who was I to interfere with, as Buddy Holly called them, true love ways?

FIVE

THE PAVILION OVERLOOKED the river and a stretch of limestone cliffs that gleamed in the sunlight. The latest chromed and finned Detroit pleasure mobiles crowded around the structure itself. The smell of grilling burgers, the ragged laughter of three- and four-year-olds, a large portable radio playing Darlene Love's "(Today I Met) The Boy I'm Going to Marry." America, of Thee I Sing.

Lucy sat on a small boulder far upslope, where a fawn stood watching her from the woods. Instead of tennis whites she now wore jeans and a yellow blouse, her blonde hair long and loose in the wind sweeping up from the river below. She smoked a cigarette with great intensity and once, just as I approached and frightened the fawn away, touched a gentle hand to her temple, as if a headache had just struck.

"Lucy."

I didn't want to frighten her. But my call was worthless. She hadn't heard me.

I walked closer. She turned, startled, and for just a moment seemed not to recognize me.

"Oh, God, Sam. It's you."

"I didn't mean to scare you."

She pointed a finger at her lovely head. "Migraine

and—don't ever tell my mother I mentioned this—my period. How's that for God's wrath?"

She'd meant the last as a joke. She'd even given me a momentary smile. But there was no humor in the tone or the smile.

"Why would God be punishing you, Lucy?"

"Because I killed David."

Wind and the sound of a grass mower somewhere and downslope the delighted screams of the pavilion kids.

"You shouldn't say things like that, Lucy. It could be dangerous."

"It's true, Sam." Her eyes coveted my face, searching for even a hint of wisdom. But I was twenty-six-year-old Sam McCain and I had no wisdom.

"It's not true, Lucy."

"He wanted to break it off. He said he was destroying my life. He said that I didn't have the strength to pull away but that he did. But I wouldn't let him." The tears came then, soft, soft as Lucy. "And they killed him. They said they would and they did."

Face in hands, sobbing now, not soft, hard, hating his killers, hating herself.

"Who said they'd kill him, Lucy?"

She raised her small bottom up from the rock and pulled three small envelopes from her back pocket. As she handed them to me, she forced herself to stop sobbing. For moments, like a child, she couldn't catch her breath. I didn't look at the envelopes until I saw that she was all right.

Crude drawings of a stick figure hanging from a noose attached to nothing. And the words "Sambo has defiled the white race and he will die for it."

All three were identical. The postmarks put them three days apart, all mailed from Cedar Rapids.

"I know who killed him, Sam, and it wasn't that stupid biker."

"Who do you think did it?"

Anger. "Goddammit, Sam, I didn't say that I *think*. I said I *know*, all right?"

"All right. You know. Then tell me."

"Rob and Nick."

Simply Rob and Nick.

There were all sorts of ways to respond to what she said. But most of them would have just agitated her further. I went with "Tell me some more."

She dug in the front of her jeans and pulled out a crumpled package of Winstons. She delicately plucked one free and then straightened it out before lighting it. The wind whipped away her first stream of smoke.

She was composed now. Hard, even. I'd never seen her this way. "Well, for one thing, they kept threatening to do it."

"Both of them?"

"Both of them. Together and separately."

"Drunk or sober?"

"Both."

"Did they ever try anything?"

Another drag from her cigarette. "David had a little motor scooter. It wouldn't do more than thirty miles an hour. He rode it back and forth between Iowa City and here on the nights when my parents wouldn't give me the car. One night, when he was coming back from my house, they were parked in the woods and then they started following. They kept running him off the road.

Scaring him. And he was scared. Then another night they got into his apartment in Iowa City and drew all kinds of terrible racist stuff on the walls."

"You sure it was them?"

"Nick Hannity bragged about it."

Fun guys, Rob and Nick.

"But killing is a long way from what you're describing."

"Nick beat him up in Iowa City one night. Badly enough that he had to stay overnight in the hospital."

"Did he go to the cops?"

"Coming from Chicago? David wasn't a big fan of cops." The sunlight revealed the freckles across her nose and cheeks. A fetching touch of prairie girl. "There wasn't much he could do. For one thing, we were both scared that the next time Rob and Nick did anything it'd be much worse."

"You couldn't tell your parents?"

"Are you kidding? They wouldn't have taken Rob's part but they would have nagged me about how this wouldn't have been happening if David wasn't a Negro."

I got out a Lucky and lighted it. "Let me say something and don't get mad."

She smiled. A genuine smile. "I'm sorry, Sam. I can be a bitch."

"You weren't a bitch. You're just understandably sad about David. But I need you to be rational and think clearly."

She nodded. "I'll try."

"I have enough to go to Cliffie with, but with the connections Rob has he'll be able to hide behind a lawyer. And besides, Cliffie has a boss now."

"Cliffie has a boss?" A half smile. "He's got to be a relative."

"He is a she. But she's not like other Sykeses. She eats with a fork and knife and never takes her dentures out at the table."

She was enjoying this diversion. "God Almighty, can such a Sykes exist?"

"Jane is her name."

"The new district attorney is a woman?"

"Not only a woman but a Brown grad. Honors from Brown and was second in her school class."

"A Sykes?"

"A Sykes. A cousin. Old Man Sykes would have preferred a Sykes male, but he couldn't find one smart enough for Dartmouth, which he's got a fondness for because of some movie he saw when he was a kid. And Old Man Sykes got her elected because he knows how tired people are of Cliffie. Who, by the way, has improved considerably since he became a hero. I've got two uncles who were falling-down drunks and they've been on the wagon for about fifteen years each. I believe people can change."

"Even Cliffie?" Then, frowning: "That's what I meant about being a bitch. We make so much fun of him it's hard to remember he's a real human being. I suppose he *can* change. But he arrested that biker so quickly—"

"His mistake. Jane's in Chicago right now at a legal convention. She's back this afternoon. And I'll bet the biker is turned loose by sundown. And I also bet that Cliffie catches hell from Jane."

"You sound like you have a lot of faith in this cousin of his, Sam."

"You will, too, when you see her."

"That means she must be pretty."

"I've only seen her from afar, as they say. Haven't spoken with her yet."

Without warning, she covered her face with her hands. "I'm sitting here on this beautiful day," she said, the words muffled by her fingers, "and David is dead. I feel guilty about it—every time I see a butterfly or a speedboat or one of those sweet little kids down there, I think it should be me who's dead—but now I'm tired, Sam. Will you just leave me alone now? Please?"

I walked downslope to my car. As I passed the pavilion, a woman came out and handed me a s'more. I spent the drive back trying to get the marshmallow goo off my fingers. But at least the good taste stayed in my mouth.

SIX

"HAVE YOU HEARD the radio in Cedar Rapids?" Judge Esme Anne Whitney snapped at me on the other end of the phone.

"Guess I haven't."

"Well, so much for this story not touching the senator."

"They named him?"

"They didn't have to. They named Lucy as a 'very good friend' of David Leeds. Said that they were coeditors of an off-campus literary magazine."

"No other implication?"

"No other implication, McCain? Do you have gravel for brains? If this is the first story, imagine what it'll be tomorrow or two days from now. They'll find people in Iowa City who'll say they were dating. They'll probably even find a few of them here."

"How long will you be in your office?"

"Aaron will be here with the car in five minutes. Then I'm going home. I need to make a very important phone call tonight on California time." I heard her lighter come ablaze. One of her numerous Gauloises. "There's not much we can do about the press now. But we can wrap this thing up as fast as possible."

"Cliffie's already arrested somebody."

"(A) You know all about Cliffie's track record. We've proved him wrong on ninety percent of his arrests. And (B) the thug has already been released. Jane Sykes is back in town, and one of the first things she did was look at the so-called evidence that Cliffie had on the man and she immediately told Cliffie to let him go."

Then I told her everything Lucy and I had discussed. "Lucy can't believe there's a Sykes who could get a degree at Brown."

"I'm told she's even an opera fan."

"She must be a Republican."

"You and your stupid Republican jokes. If you ever grow up, you'll be one of us, McCain. I promise you that."

She rarely said good-bye and this late afternoon was no exception. She simply slammed the receiver down.

"FAR AS I'M CONCERNED, my brother died because of that colored boy. No other reason at all."

Will Neville was watching a *Maverick* rerun when I knocked on the screen door of his apartment on the upper floor of an old house whose stucco had mostly fallen away.

Now I sat in a living room filled with furniture that looked as old as the house. I sat on a horsehair sofa. He had a big Cubs pennant on one wall and a Hawkeye pennant on another. There were cardboard boxes everywhere, overflowing with things as various as kitchen utensils and dusty, brittle-looking shoes. It was one of those suffocating little prisons, his apartment, with faded rose wallpaper and tiny mouse droppings littered across the scraped hardwood floor.

"Just moved in, huh?"

"No. Why?"

I glanced around the room again. "I was just wondering, all the boxes."

He shrugged sturdy shoulders. "Just haven't had time to unpack them yet. Sometimes I live here and sometimes I live with my older brothers in Chicago. Not that it's any of your business."

He wore a Stanley Kowalski T-shirt and a pair of work pants. He had a belly that could have accommodated a set of twins. He was hairy in a dirty way. I wondered if he'd ever considered shaving his arms.

"Like I said, far as I'm concerned, my brother died because of that colored boy. No other reason at all."

"Why do you say that?"

"Why do I say that? My brother didn't have no enemies. Everybody liked him. Some bastard followed Leeds out to my brother's place and decided to kill both of them. To confuse people." He made a face and then noisily gulped half a can of the A&P beer he'd been swigging all along. He made everything official by belching. "You knew my brother."

"Sort of." I'd actually represented him in a Peeping Tom incident a few years earlier. I felt he was falsely accused in that one. But by the time the trial was over, I'd come to feel he was a pretty dark guy.

"Well, then you'd know, nobody would want to kill him."

"He ever talk about knowing David Leeds?"

"Said Leeds stopped out there a couple of times."

"He say why?"

"Said he wanted to learn about photography. I

suppose they have colored photographers in Chicago, you know, for the colored trade and all. I didn't think nothing of it, but I wasn't real happy with him spending much time with Leeds."

"Had you ever met Leeds?"

"No, but you know how people are. They see you spending a lot of time with a colored boy, they start to wonder about you."

"I guess I don't understand."

"You know, they start thinking maybe something's wrong with you. Think maybe you can't get white friends or something." He smirked. "Especially hangin' around a colored boy that gives dance lessons."

"He did anything he could for college money."

"Still and all, a boy who teaches dance lessons? Ain't real manly."

The smirk again. "You wouldn't see me givin' no dance lessons."

It was too tempting. Instead I said, "I see. Did your brother seem happy lately?"

"Happy? No shit, he seemed happy. He come into this job over in Des Moines. Some studio named Brilliance I think it was. Brilliant or Brilliance, one of those. Said that their best photographer got sick and they had this real important job they had to do fast. And they needed somebody as good as the sick guy. So they called my brother. He made so much money on it he slipped me a hundred bucks so I could get caught up with my light bill and shit like that. But that's what I mean, the kinda guy who would slip you a hundred, who'd want to kill him? I'm just glad my folks aren't alive to have to see this. And like I said, it's all this

Leeds's fault. You get a colored boy pokin' around a white gal, you got trouble. And that's just what he got, ain't it? Trouble."

SEVEN

AFTER DRIVING TWO BLOCKS, I realized I was probably being followed. I say probably because there were an awful lot of white 1961 Plymouth Valiants on the road. I was pretty sure that this was the Valiant that had been at Neville's cabin the night before. But I needed a closer look at the license plate. Once I got one and confirmed it was the Valiant I wanted, I let him follow me for another three blocks.

When we got to a red light, I yanked on the emergency brake and jumped out of my ragtop. I brought one of the two guns in my glove compartment with me.

He was slow to realize what I was going to do. The corner we were at was empty except for us. The small shops on both sides of the street were closed. The only activity was half a block away at the Dairy Queen. It was dusk.

He started putting his Valiant in reverse, but before he got anywhere, I shoved my .45 through his open window and put it right to his head.

"Pull over to the curb."

"What for?"

"Pull over to the curb."

"You bastard. Nobody pulls a gun on me."

"I just did. Now pull over to the curb."

I could see he was considering just flooring the Valiant and peeling away. But then he had to gauge how crazy I might be. You never know with people who pull guns.

He pulled over to the curb.

"Now turn off the engine and step out of the car."

"You know, a cop could drive by here anytime, asshole, and your ass would be grass."

"Turn off the engine and step out of the car."

"You're gonna regret this."

"Not as much as you are." But he finally turned off the engine. I opened the door for him. He stepped out.

Then I plucked his car keys from his hand.

And that was when I shot him right in the face. It was my mood, I guess. I didn't even worry about the consequences. I felt my life was at an end and nothing mattered.

"You bastard," he said.

He looked pretty pathetic there in his tight black suit with the pegged trousers and gold tie bar and porkpie hat, a denizen of a Chicago twist club if I'd ever seen one. And all that water running down his face.

"A squirt gun?"

"Yeah, I had a gunsmith modify a squirt gun so it'd look like the real thing." I nodded to the DQ down the street. "Let's go."

"YOU KNOW, they keep introducing all these new flavors and cones and malts and stuff. But if you ask me, you can't beat your basic chocolate sundae. How's your cone?"

"How's my cone? This is how my cone is."

We were sitting on a bench on the far side of the DQ so we could call each other foul names without offending all the moms and kids lined up for treats at the counters.

He took his cone and threw it hard against the blacktop parking lot. "That's how my cone is. Now give me back my car keys."

"You don't want me to squirt you again, do you?" I was aggravating the hell out of him and enjoying myself. Life was good again. I would find the Right Woman after all.

I pulled my wallet out and showed him my two pieces of identification. One was private investigator. The other was court investigator.

"The last one's the one you have to worry about. I have the power to arrest you." I decided not to point out that every other American citizen has the same right. "So let's cut the bullshit and you tell me who you are and what you were doing out at Neville's cabin the other night."

"And if I don't?"

"And if you don't, I take you right to jail."

"For what?"

"For being at a murder scene and not reporting it."

And that was when one of Cliffie's finest pulled up next to where our cars had been pulled in, not with any great talent for careful parking, to the curb.

The car had the red lights flashing but no siren.

"Get over here, McCain. You're getting a ticket." He was a young guy named O'Brien and he was ticket-happy.

I made the mistake of turning to O'Brien to explain

to him that I was working on a case for the judge when the man next to me damn near vaulted up from the bench and started running away.

"I'll be back!" I shouted to O'Brien.

And O'Brien shouted: "Where the hell you think you're going?"

There were three of us—Mr. Twist, me, and O'Brien, running across the parking lot toward the busy avenue that ran adjacent to the DQ.

And for a block, it was really a race. None of us was in danger of becoming a track star. None of us was in danger of becoming graceful. None of us was in danger of catching the others.

The sidewalk we were racing down was no beauty. A lot of cracks, a lot of places where the concrete had stove in to create jagged points.

So we stumbled a lot. And shouted curses at the other guys because somehow the stumbling was their fault.

We attracted our share of attention from the traffic streaming by at 40 mph. There was something about three grown men in pursuit of each other. And even more, there was something about a cop in uniform waving his gun in the air and shouting "Stop or I'll shoot!"

You don't get this kind of realistic TV on *Dragnet,* that's for sure.

When it happened, it was over so quickly I had to wonder if what I'd just witnessed had actually taken place.

Mr. Twist had jumped from the sidewalk to the avenue and attempted to race across the street.

Insane on his part.

Cars going by fast enough and close enough that they were starting to resemble those streaming photographs where everything is a streaking blur.

And then he just leapt into the traffic stream.

But a streamlined, new two-tone blue Oldsmobile slowed him down instantly by hitting him at 40 mph or so and then punting him to the opposite curb, where he landed—from what I could see—next to a fire hydrant.

He'd screamed while still in midair. Or at least I thought I'd heard him scream. Maybe it was screeching tires, all the drivers trying to halt speeding cars.

The white-haired man in the Olds was out of his car and running to the opposite curb before O'Brien and I, who now stood side by side, could even start into the street.

O'Brien started using his traffic whistle and, holding his left arm up to stop traffic completely, gave us a chance to get to the mystery man.

I've never had any interest in seeing human beings ripped apart or smashed up inside and turned into a big blood-leaking chunk of human hamburger. A lot of people seem to regard a glimpse of stuff like this as a treat.

So I wasn't all that hot on seeing what was left of our feckless friend who tried to outmaneuver tons of speeding Detroit iron.

But he didn't look that bad.

His right arm was obviously broken. He was bleeding through a busted nose and ripped-up lips. And his left foot had somehow lost its shoe. But no human hamburger.

"Take over. I'll call for an ambulance." O'Brien started running back to his car.

"Stay back."

The crowd was small for now. Maybe fifteen people from cars and the DQ. In a few minutes it would look like a movie opening.

Comments:

"Is he dead?"

"He looks dead."

"Hell, he isn't dead."

"Oh, yeah, what're you, a doctor now?"

I knelt next to him. His eyes flickered open a few times, but despite the moans, I wasn't sure he was conscious.

I checked his wrist pulse and his neck pulse.

"How's his pulse, mister?"

Might as well answer. "Pretty good. Better than I would've thought, in fact."

O'Brien, breathless, sweaty, was back. "Ambulance on the way." He haunched down next to me. "Who is he?"

"I don't know."

"You're sitting at the Dairy Queen talking to him and you don't know?"

I didn't want to discuss it with eavesdroppers around.

A siren worked its way from the hospital five blocks away, that sad scary sound. The nuns always had us say a prayer for the person in need whenever we heard a siren. Probably not all that bad an idea.

Two more uniformed cops.

"Let's go back to our cars," I said to O'Brien. I wasn't going to tell him much, just enough to explain why I didn't know the injured man's name.

By the time we got back to the DQ, he seemed to be satisfied that this was all the result of some guy following me around in the white Valiant for reasons I didn't understand.

He said, when we came into the stark, bug-swarmed fluorescent light of the DQ, "Think I'll have a cone. You want one?"

"Nah. Got an appointment I need to keep."

"Guess I won't give you a ticket, after all."

"Appreciate it."

And then I was gone.

EIGHT

THE HANNITY HOUSE WAS one of the new ranch styles that sat in scornful superiority above all the little Levittown-like boxes in the valley below.

The boxes had been built back in '49 and '50 when the American Dream everybody had fought for in the war seemed to be coming true.

But in a decade, the boxes had begun to show the perils of houses built so hastily and so ineptly. The pastel exteriors that had shone like dewy flowers in morning light had faded. Windows had dislodged from cheap frames and sliding tracks. And the yards the developers had promised never quite came to look like yards, just thin stretches of grass on dirt.

But moon shadow was merciful. As my ragtop climbed the winding hill leading to the imposing homes at the top, I was able to remember how much I'd always wanted to live in one of those boxes when I was in my early teens. We'd moved from the Knolls, where the poorest of working families lived, to the glamour of a housing development. I could still remember a kid telling me that many of the homes there had actual extension telephones. That's right, more than one phone in the house so you could talk to your friends—and hopefully that someday girlfriend—in the privacy of your own room. For some stupid reason the extension phone had struck me as an invention much superior to that of the airplane or medical advances.

I'd never dreamed big enough to think that I'd someday live up on the hill above the boxes. The boxes, with a real laundry room for Mom, a basement shop for all of Dad's tools, and a sunny room for my often sad little sister— who could want more than a housing development house?

A yellow Lincoln was parked in the driveway of the Hannity house. From inside, fairly loud, came Sinatra singing Jerome Kern—as much as I loved rock, I was beginning to learn my American popular composers— and tinny martini laughter.

I pulled up, killed the lights, and then watched as the double garage door ground its way upward, revealing two cars parked inside, one a black Lincoln and one a 1962 buff-blue Chevrolet.

My ragtop sat directly behind the Chevrolet. Nick Hannity was just about to climb into the Chevrolet when he turned and saw my car.

In the grainy garage light, almost in silhouette, he looked bigger than ever. Football hero, tormentor of Lucy Williams and David Leeds, and now insolent swaggerer making his way to my car.

No way was I going to let him trap me inside. I opened the door and got out.

As he approached, he said, "You're trespassing, asshole."

"Wrong-o, Hannity. I'm a licensed investigator and I'm investigating. Legally."

"Yeah? Well, then I'm gonna illegally throw your ass off of my property."

When I was growing up, even though I was small, I always figured for some balmy reason that I was just naturally stronger and tougher than kids younger than me. And most of them seemed to go along with it. I wasn't a bully, but in the way of the playground and the backyard, I usually got younger kids to do what I told them to.

Then one sixth-grade autumn day when I was walking home with my friend Carl Sears, generally known as a puncher, some stupid kid in fifth grade started mouthing off behind us. His prey seemed to be Carl. I wondered if the stupid kid knew who Carl was.

Couple more blocks, Carl just sort of laughing at it. And then Carl turning without warning and hooking a right hand into the kid's face with enough force to knock the stupid kid back a good three or four feet.

An easy, clean victory for Carl.

Except it wasn't. Because the kid picked himself up and proceeded to beat the holy hell out of Carl, thus ending my personal myth of age mattering in a fight.

Now here was Hannity, a college senior probably four years younger, just about ready to take me apart. Age didn't matter, my badge didn't matter, whatever status I had as an associate of Judge Whitney's didn't matter.

He was closing in on me and he had every right to think—to know—that I was afraid of him.

He was tough, but he wasn't subtle. He spent too much time bringing his left hand up. In those seconds I was able to plant the tip of my shoe right in his crotch.

I had the extreme pleasure of watching him fall to the ground, clutch his crotch, and cry out in pain.

"You son of a bitch," he said. "I'm gonna tell my dad."

But Dad was already running toward us. He obviously had a keen paternal ear. He'd heard his son's cry.

As soon as he saw his son on the ground, he let out a yelp that combined fear and rage in equal parts.

But as he leaned down to help his son to his feet, Hannity started the painful climb on his own. "I don't need any help."

"What's going on here, Nick?" Bill Hannity said.

"Ask that asshole over there."

He looked over at me. He was a beefier version of his beefy son, a financial consultant in Cedar Rapids who tended to dress in California casual as often as possible: sport shirt, custom-fit slacks, and a tan collected from visits to three or four sunny climes a year.

He was also much smoother than his son. "Are you beating up children now, McCain?"

There were two warring groups at the town's lone country club. One was run by the judge, the other by him.

"Yeah, I usually kick the shit out of ten-year-olds a couple times a week."

Now that Junior was on his feet, Bill said, "Are you all right, Nick?"

"He really hurt me, Dad."

Back to me: "What the hell do you think you're doing, McCain?"

I shrugged: "It was either that or let him take me apart. He started coming at me. I didn't have a lot of choices."

"He's just a college kid."

"Yeah, and he's got forty pounds on me and is one of the biggest bullies in town. As you might have guessed, since he's been in court four or five times on assault charges."

Nick, even though he was still wincing from time to time, started toward me. But my words had cooled Bill off at least temporarily.

"What are you doing on my property?"

"Investigating. I'm licensed, you'll remember."

"Damned Esme." He shook his sleek gray head. "Investigating what, may I ask?"

"Trying to find out if your son was involved in the murders of the two men last night."

"That colored boy? My God, McCain, what the hell would my son have to do with that?"

"He has a history of harassing Leeds."

"You're a liar. And besides, I was with my girlfriend Nancy Adams last night." Nick started at me again. Bill put a formidable restraining arm across his son's chest.

"Be quiet, Nick. What're you talking about, McCain?"

I told him what Lucy had told me, about how his son and Rob Anderson had treated Leeds on several occasions.

"He's lying, Dad."

"There's a witness," I said.

"Nick wouldn't do anything like that. He's got a temper but—"

"Tell that to Lucy Williams. She knows better."

"That bitch," Nick said.

Bill Hannity's expression changed. He seemed to consider the possibility, for the first time, that maybe something was going on here.

"Go in the house, Nick."

"Dad, this little jerk kicked me in the crotch."

"In the house, Nick. Now."

His quiet authority impressed me. He'd handled himself pretty well, considering that he'd found his son writhing on the driveway.

Nick gave me the big bad glare and muttered all the usual curses just loudly enough that I could hear them. But then he turned and hobbled his way back to the house. I hadn't meant to kick him that hard but I probably wasn't going to cry myself to sleep about it.

Bill Hannity took a cigarette from the pack of Camels in his blue sport shirt, flamed it with a golden shaft of expensive lighter, and said, "Is he really in trouble?"

"Right now it's hard to say."

He made a face. "That damned temper of his. I suppose I was just as bad when I was his age. But you didn't have to kick him that hard."

"He didn't have to charge me, either."

He took a drag off his cigarette and blew the smoke up toward the clean nuggets of stars. This was the air of privilege up here, the warmth and safety of the lights in the wide windows of the ranch house, the expensive cars on the drive, and again the swagger of rich-people laughter fluttering up into the sky like sleek golden birds.

"I'll talk to him. Do I need a lawyer yet?"

"See what Nick says first."

He arced his cigarette into the air with all the finesse of a street-corner punk. A meteor shower erupted when cigarette met lawn.

He put his hand to his head and sighed. "A white girl who comes from a good family going out with a colored boy. It had to be trouble. It had to be."

He didn't shake my hand but he chucked me on the arm and said, "Thanks for being honest with me, McCain."

Then he went back inside with his own class of people.

NINE

THERE'S A SMALL CAFÉ half a block from the courthouse that, at night anyway, resembles the café made famous by Edward Hopper. You rarely see more than two people at the counter and I don't recall ever seeing anybody occupy any of the four booths. The man in the white T-shirt and apron behind the counter speaks a language nobody's ever quite been able to identify. And the faded posters on the walls advertise obscure singers from the '30s who appeared at a dance hall closed down in the late '40s.

I go there sometimes when I can't sleep and I can't even tell you why. The old songs on the jukebox, the silent people sipping coffee at the counter, the counter-man talking angrily on the phone in that strange language—it's our own little corner of the Twilight Zone.

Tonight, though, I got a surprise. Not only were there at least six people at the counter, there was also somebody occupying one of the booths. And that was the second surprise. The occupant was none other than the new district attorney, Jane Sykes.

She wore a white silk blouse and a navy blue suit. With her golden hair swept back into a chignon and a cigarette burning in the ashtray, she had a certain chic that didn't get in the way of her melancholy aura.

And there was yet another surprise. When I got to her booth, carrying the cup of coffee I'd bought, I saw the title of the book she was reading: *The Stranger* by Albert Camus.

"Miss Sykes."

An expression of irritation drew her chic face tight. She'd been engrossed in the book.

"Yes?" Then: "Oh." Then a long and silken hand angled up toward me. I took it and we shook. "You're Sam McCain."

"Yes."

"Please. Sit down."

"Looks as if I've dragged you away from your reading."

"You did." The smile was a beam that brought peace and wisdom to the entire universe. "But sit down and we'll talk lawyer stuff."

"You always work this late?" I said as I sat down.

"My first eight years were in the Cook County office. You've heard of Chicago? Seven days of twelve hours a day sometimes. This is nice so far. Only a couple of those twelve-hour days." She raised her cup as if in a toast. "Plus the coffee's better here."

"You actually like this place?"

"You know who Edward Hopper is?"

I laughed. "That's who I think of every time I walk in here."

"I don't know much about art but I had a husband who did. And there was a traveling Hopper show at the Art Institute for a month. I went every day. It was like a religious experience."

"Same way here."

"He explained something to me—about myself." She smiled that smile again. "The trouble is I can't articulate it, what he explained to me. Not even to myself."

I must have looked transfixed. I sure felt that way.

"Want me to read your mind, Sam?"

"My mind?"

"Yes, I'm pretty sure you have one." She tapped a long, red-tipped finger against her perfect forehead. "Want me to read it?"

"Uh, sure."

"You're thinking how could anybody with the name Sykes know anything about Edward Hopper."

"Hey, c'mon." But I knew I was flushing. Of course I'd had that thought two or three times since sitting down here. "Why would I think anything like that?"

"Because my family has its share of dim bulbs, as I'll admit. Not to mention criminals. But they're not stupid, they're just uneducated. And they're uneducated because they're too lazy to learn. They look at 'book learning,' as they call it, as effete and dull. The women as well as the men, unfortunately." She stubbed out a Viceroy and tamped another one from her pack. "So let's be clear about this. I'm well aware of my family's faults. That's why my dad fled to Chicago as soon as he could. He wanted to be educated. But the big war got in his way and he got wounded in such a way that he has these terrible memory lapses. But he made sure that I did everything he couldn't do."

"You must be something in court. You just spoke everything in perfect sentences."

"I wasn't trying to dazzle you, Sam. I was trying to make a point. You and I will be bumping up against each other in a lot of different situations. I know you work for the judge and you know I'm a Sykes, but that's no reason we can't be friends. You know, in Chicago, lawyers for the prosecution and lawyers for the defense can actually be friends." She had an easy touch with wry comments.

"And in a small town, I like the idea of having a friend who knows who Edward Hopper is. But—" She folded her hands on the table and looked at me directly. This particular gray-eyed gaze had to be a killer in court. "But whatever your feelings about any of the Sykeses, including Clifford, I want you to keep them to yourself. I'm well aware of his shortcomings, and one of my first priorities is to straighten out the police department. But he's my flesh and blood and I know a side of him you don't. So, no Cliff jokes, no Cliff jibes. If he does something that conflicts with the law, let me know and I'll take care of it. Otherwise, the subject of Clifford is off-limits. All right?"

"Breathtaking. God, I'm afraid to go up against you in court."

"I'm serious about it, Sam."

"I know you are. But that didn't take anything away from the presentation."

She sat back in the booth. Yawned. Covered her mouth with that long, graceful hand. "Sorry. I guess I'm not as young as I used to be."

"Ancient."

"Thirty-one next month." Thank God the smile came back. "That's almost five years older than you."

"How'd you know that?"

"You think I didn't research every attorney in the county when I came out here?"

"Do I get to research you?"

"Be my guest. You know how old I am. My husband divorced me four years ago because of all the hours I put in and because I didn't want children. Now I think maybe I would like to have a child, but the problem is I haven't met anybody I'd like to get serious with, let alone get married to. As for my time in the DA's office, I held the highest position ever held by a woman in the Cook County legal establishment. I'm slim but it's becoming a battle to stay that way. And of all the lawyers in town, you're the one most interesting to me."

She tapped the finger where a wedding ring had once resided. "You're single. That means you can show me the town."

"Such as it is."

"Such as it is."

Then, without warning, she was gathering up her materials and sweeping herself out of the booth. "Want to walk me to my hotel? I haven't found a place yet."

"Sure."

I hadn't walked a woman home in some time. And I liked it.

"This must be quite a change from Chicago."

"It is. But I'm enjoying it. I'll like it even better when I'm moved in somewhere."

As we walked I felt connected again. Girl-connected with all its rich erotic promise.

And then we were standing in front of the hotel, three wide steps up to a pair of revolving doors and a surprisingly comely interior.

She extended her hand and we shook. "Thanks, Sam. I've really enjoyed meeting you."

And then she was gone. I tumbled down into the womanless darkness that had been my home since Mary had found out that she couldn't marry me. Her husband Wes, who'd left her for another woman, had gotten Mary pregnant with their third child, unbeknownst to both of them. Since Wes had gotten dumped by his new girlfriend, he saw the wisdom of returning to Mary. She didn't believe in abortion. She would have the baby— had already had the baby girl, in fact—and Mary and Wes would try again to save their marriage.

I went for a long, melancholy ride in my ragtop, and then I went home to feed the cats.

TEN

"I PLAY A PICKLE, SAM," Samantha said on the other end of the phone. "A network commercial, too. The residuals should be really good."

Samantha, a very appealing copper-haired young woman from right here in Black River Falls, had been in Los Angeles. Couple of years older than me, a small legal infraction known as shoplifting being the way we'd met, she finally decided that maybe "everybody" was right, she should try Hollywood before it was too late. She did the impossible. She got me to keep her three cats for her, Tasha, Crystal, and Tess. I was previously a cat-disliker. Not hater. But disliker.

Until I got her cats. And they became my cats by default.

She checks in three or four times a year, usually when she has news of a commercial or a bit part in a movie or a TV show or a stage play. I've never summoned the nerve to recommend to her one of my three or four favorite novels, *They Shoot Horses, Don't They?* by Horace McCoy. It's the most scathing of all the Hollywood novels about people who trek out there filled with Cinemascope dreams about the gilded life that will be theirs.

To date, according to her count, she's had more than

a dozen jobs, slept with three bona fide movie stars, endured two failed marriages, one miscarriage and two abortions, and has spent a good deal of her modest income seeing a shrink who has convinced her that the sex they have is a vital part of the therapeutic process, something she admitted while stoned on marijuana and wine.

She checks in on her cats the way a really bad parent would check in on children she never sees, all effusive stagecraft about how much she misses them, thinks about them, even dreams about them. I'm sort of the adoptive cat parent now. Or the cat nanny.

After Samantha and I said our good-byes, I took off my clothes, grabbed a beer from the fridge, turned on the TV just for noise, and then saw the piece of paper by the door. I went over and picked it up and brought it back to the couch.

The cats read it with me, Tasha in my lap, Crystal and Tess on the back of the couch, reading over my shoulder.

Sam—
I saw something last night that might have some-thing to do with those murders. I'm actually kind of scared about it. That's why I stopped by. I'm staying at a girlfriend's trailer tonight. Her number is 407-5411. I'd appreciate a call. Don't worry how late it is.
Rachael Todd

A client of mine in a spooky divorce. A husband so abusive he'd once chased her through the woods with a fire ax. For which he is still serving some well-deserved time.

A Knolls kid, like me, Rachael had dropped out of school in tenth grade and taken up with the Road Devils, some local bikers who fashioned themselves after the Hell's Angels. At first they'd been poor imitations. But by now they were serious criminals: car theft (the cars driven to Chicago where they were repainted and their registration numbers filed off, sold at auction to used-car lots), arson-for-hire, and numerous charges of assault and battery. Judge Whitney had sent a few of them up, in fact.

Rachael wasn't especially attractive physically except for her enormous breasts. I'd always felt sorry for her. Nobody'd ever paid her any attention until her breasts sprouted, and then she was reduced to something of a joke by boys and girls alike. I suppose hanging out with the bikers gave her the sense of belonging she'd never found at school.

I'd lost touch with her since the divorce decree two years ago, though I wondered about her occasionally. She'd always be one of those sad-eyed kids nobody at school had ever bothered to bestow humanity on.

I dialed the number. One thing she wasn't was a hysteric. If she thought she'd seen something, she'd seen something.

No answer.

I dialed and redialed right up to when the yawning finally overcame me and I turned off the TV and went to bed.

It was just before 6:30 the next morning when the

clock radio next to my bed came on with the news that a body identified as that of Rachael Todd had been found on the highway, the victim of an apparent hit-and-run.

PART TWO

ELEVEN

WHENEVER I WANT to find out what I really think about something, I go to the barbershop, the same barbershop I've been going to since my mom quit cutting my hair when I turned three. The two men who ran the shop since the 1920s have retired now, but the other characters are pretty much the same.

The men who collect here, whether they need a haircut or not, are a good cross-section of small-town folks: farmers, blue-collar workers, merchants, a newspaperman or two, and a fair number of retirees.

Pipes, cigarettes, cigars are smoked. Dirty jokes are told. Gossip is exchanged. And politics are argued.

I happened to need a haircut, so after visiting the morgue to learn what I could about Rachael Todd's death, I spent part of the early morning sitting in a barber's chair, soaking up not only the commentary but also the wonderful timeless scents of the barbershop—the hot foam for shaving, the aftershaves, the hair tonics, the powder, the smell of the bristles in the whisk broom when the barber is cleaning off your neck and shoulders.

The talk itself this particular morning took a roundabout way of becoming political, traveling from the particular to the general—from the murders of Leeds and Neville to the civil rights struggle on the tube every night.

The only thing that didn't figure into the mix was Rachael Todd's death. They'd heard about it but they didn't know yet that it had some undetermined connection to the murders.

"LANDED AT an odd angle," the new county medical examiner showed me after tugging out the drawer in which Rachael resided. "Broke her neck."

His name was Dr. Henry Renning and his duties were part time. He had his own practice to tend to the rest of the time. He was best known for wearing one of the most hilariously lousy toupees in town history and for driving a 1951 cherry MG that everybody, including me, envied the hell out of.

I hadn't seen Rachael much since handling her divorce. She'd put on considerable weight. In death, at least, she appeared to be much older than her calendar years. She looked sexless now, and she'd been one of those women who made up with an erotic air what she lacked in looks.

"Her blood alcohol was nearly three times the legal limit. The way the accident looks to have happened, I'm not even sure the driver was sure he'd hit anybody. It's pretty dark on that stretch of highway and she might just have lurched into his headlights."

"I didn't know she was a drinker."

Renning nodded. His rug moved a half inch down his forehead. "The woman who identified her, her sister, said that Rachael here was in AA and had been up to that clinic for alcoholics in Mason City. Twice, in fact."

First her husband had beaten her up with his fists. Then she'd beaten herself up with liquor.

I became aware of where I was. The bodies in the drawers. The terrible cold stench of the place. The hum of gurney wheels as corpses were moved around, the efficiency of it all as depressing as the sight of a man and woman weeping on the other side of a glass door as I'd come in. Weeping silently because I couldn't hear them, a scene from an ancient silent movie.

But mostly I was aware of poor Rachael, the left side of her face almost black with bruising from her accident. And various other bruises and small cuts up and down her body. Meat now. Just human meat. I wish Dylan Thomas had been right about death not having dominion. But that was just a poet's fancy to put up against eternal darkness. Death has plenty of dominion. Plenty.

"Got a suicide I need to check out," Renning said, his toupee looking like a squirrel sprawled over his bald pate. "We about done here, Sam?"

IF THERE WERE A LIST of Top Ten Barbershop Topics over the past few years it would include the birth control pill ("Shit, why didn't they have somethin' like that when I was young; McCain, your generation's got it knocked!"); the Berlin Wall ("Who gives a shit? After what the Krauts did, screw 'em!"); Ernest Hemingway ("All the money and all the broads that guy had and he kills himself?"); the recent trip by Rick Paulson to the Playboy Club in Chicago, the first of our townspeople to enter those sacred doors ("Hefner just walks around in his tuxedo with that damn pipe of his and the gals are all over him!"); and the recent murder of Medgar Evers ("I think the colored people are pushin' it pretty hard these days but I don't hold with no murder.").

"That wife of Williams's didn't look so snotty when I seen her at the post office yesterday, I'll tell you that much."

"'Bout time we got a Democrat in there, anyway."

"I had a daughter seein' a colored boy, I'd whip her ass good."

"I can tell you I'd take a couple of colored boys I used to serve with in Korea over some of the white boys around here."

"They say in France they treat Negroes just like white people."

"Yeah, well, that's the French. We had to save their ass in the big war and they never have thanked us."

"I don't want to be nowhere around 'em. I don't like lookin' at them or talkin' to them or even thinkin' about them."

"Segregation's good for them. They do better when they're with their own."

"Ike was the one who named that son of a bitch Warren to head up the Supreme Court. He's the one who started all this."

"My son in Des Moines says my grandkids go to school with colored kids and they all get along just fine."

"Look at Sammy Davis. He don't care who knows he's married to a white woman."

"Well, they fought in the war just like I did. They shouldn't get shoved around the way they do. You see them little kids when they get them hoses turned on 'em? I went south one time and you can keep it. Didn't care for one bit of it."

"I'll take Nat 'King' Cole any day. He's my kind of colored man. A gentleman."

"I hear a couple of those bikers really had it in for that Leeds kid."

Somehow, if you listened long enough and carefully enough, you heard the kind of prairie debate that was going on, in a more sophisticated way perhaps, all across the country. You heard the men good and true and the men confused and struggling and the men who hated, one or two of them who might even be capable of violence against Negroes in the great wrong moment.

And once in a while, no matter what the subject was—and it could be anything from did Marilyn Monroe really commit suicide to why Roger Maris really was entitled to that home run record after all— once in a while you really learned something specific and useful.

In this case, it had to do with David Leeds.

"Hey, Karl, where'd you hear that?" I asked just as Mike was using the whisk broom on me.

"About the bikers and the Leeds kid?"

"Yeah."

"Out to Savio's, getting a tune-up. One of the bikers was in there. The one wears the bandana around his head like an Indian? Name's De Ruse, you know the one I mean? After he left, Savio told me that when De Ruse was drunk he talked a lot about killing Leeds. He doesn't go for white gals and Negroes gettin' together. Savio said he saw De Ruse out in that area near those cabins when he was driving home around the time Neville and Leeds got killed."

"He really said that about De Ruse wanting to kill him?"

"He sure did."

One of the old gents laughed. "You're forgetting you're talkin' to a private investigator, Karl." And then the inevitable: "I always thought Mike Hammer was taller'n you, McCain."

"Yeah," I said. "But I'm a lot handsomer."

That got the kind of laughs and smiles a wise man uses as his exit line. Old vaudeville truism.

"Hey, McCain, didn't one of them bikers get arrested already?"

"Yeah, but as usual Cliffie arrested the wrong one."

I got another laugh at that one.

TWELVE

"SO WHAT'LL IT BE?" the cutie in the pink ruffled blouse and matching pink Capri pants asked me when I was two steps across the threshold of Gotta Dance Studio! She had dimples you could hide quarters in and happy little breasts that said, "Glad to see you." You could tell she hadn't worked here long. Chick Curtis hadn't been able to browbeat all happiness out of her yet.

She asked her question while she was still walking across the shining hardwood floor where instructors and students came together.

"You can see our list right up there on the wall. You can learn any three dances today for only nineteen ninety-five. I'm Glory, by the way."

The list was long if nothing else, and carefully hand-lettered on a white length of cardboard.

The Stroll
The Twist
The Monkey
The Jerk
The Watusi
The Mashed Potato
The Shimmy-Shimmy

The Dog
The Pony

"You look like you'd be a good dancer," she said.

"How can you tell?"

"Oh, you know, just the way you move." She seemed flustered, as if nobody had ever questioned her ability to spot good dancers. I could see why Chick had hired her. Even in her early twenties she'd retained a bit of the innocence and freshness of a much younger girl. How anybody as seedy as Chick had ever come by her, I was afraid to guess. (WHITE SEX SLAVERY IN AMERICA! the supermarket tabloid had cried last week.)

"And there're a lot more dances, too, on a sheet I can give you." Then: "Oh, darn!"

She ran over to a bulletin board filled with black-and-white Polaroids of couples who'd become Chick's Cool Ones. The odd thing was that most of the Cool Ones appeared to be in their forties and fifties. Well-dressed, middle-class folks clearly trying to capture the Kennedy mystique, Jackie Kennedy having been filmed on dozens of chi-chi dance floors twisting the night away with movie stars, political figures, and various members of the Kennedy clan. So now the Lincoln and Cadillac doctors and CEOs and real estate rich of the Midwest were rushing to grab a little bit of that Camelot luster for themselves.

I tried not to stare at her friendly little bottom as she bent to right a photo that was falling off the bulletin board. I would learn anything she cared to teach me, even, God forbid, the shimmy-shimmy.

"There," she said, pushing the red thumbtack in, "Mr. and Mrs. Winnans sure wouldn't like to see their picture on the floor."

A sexy version of Sandra Dee, she turned back to me. I probably wasn't more than seven years older than she was. But there was a chasm separating us. "So have you decided?"

"I'm sorry. I'm sort of here on business."

"Well, we're a business."

"I know. But I'm here on a different kind of business. I need to see Chick."

"Oh, you can't!"

"I can't?"

"I mean, my dad's been out of town for a week and won't be back until the weekend."

"Your dad is Chick Curtis?" I tried to keep the shock out of my voice.

"Uh-huh. Isn't that cool? He'd always teach all the kids at my parties how to dance. Are you a friend of his?"

"Well, we've done business together on occasion." Meaning I'd been able to blackmail him into giving me information from time to time. I'd had several clients who'd had problems with Chick and had learned a whole lot about him. He was the forward flank of the Quad Cities mob, which was, of course, the forward flank of the Chicago mob. With two wartime boot camps to prey on, they'd been able to take over all the prostitution and gentler kinds of drugs. They still hadn't touched heroin. Once you started playing with heroin, the feds took special note of you. Why bother with smack when you could make just as much with your other enterprises, including, of late, some mighty fine counterfeiting that extended all the way to Denver. Chick himself stuck to laundering mob money through dance studios, dry cleaners, roller rinks, construction companies, even, one hears, a group of religious book-stores throughout the Midwest.

"My name's Sam McCain."

"Oh. I think maybe he's mentioned you."

"Maybe you could help me."

"Me?" she said, as if nobody had ever asked anything of her before but to look fetching and just a wee bit dense.

"Did you hear about David Leeds being murdered?"

That little face reflected grief as well as happiness. "I'm trying not to think about it until I get off work because I don't want to be crying in front of customers all day."

"He worked here."

"Yes. Everybody liked him. Even my dad who doesn't like—you know, colored people all that much. But David needed money for college so he came in three nights a week. He was very personable and he knew all the dances. I think it was kind of a lark for him, you know? Except for all the jokes about how Negroes have natural rhythm and all that."

"That made him angry?"

"Not angry so much as—hurt. You could see it in his eyes then. The people who come in here are usually very nice and they were careful about what they said to David. But every once in a while somebody would make a joke like that and he'd kind of freeze up and just get this look on his face."

"Sad."

"Yes, sad. More than angry."

"So nobody really picked on him?"

The phone rang. It sat inside a glassed-in office. "Just a sec."

I hadn't thought about that. Teaching all those *American Bandstand* dances to white people, you'd just be setting yourself up for mean jokes. But Leeds seemed to be a serious young man who wanted a good future, so he did what he had to to get money. And a lot of folks would probably think they were just making friendly jokes, not intending to hurt his feelings at all. But it was hard to watch Sammy Davis Jr. on TV for exactly that reason. The only things people seemed capable of saying to him were race jokes. Very few were really ugly jokes, but they made it clear that to them Sammy wasn't of the same species—separate and apart. Only occasionally when you were watching him would you see that split second of pain, of humiliation. Hard to enjoy his act when you sensed that there was so much grief under all that showbiz laughter.

"Mrs. Paulson," Glory said when she came back. "Listen, why don't we sit down over at that table? I'll be on my feet for the rest of the day and night."

Once we were seated, once I'd declined her offer of either coffee or soda pop, she said, "I didn't mean to give you the impression that there wasn't any trouble. There was. Just not with our dancing people."

"There was trouble?"

"The bikers would sit outside and roar their engines and call him names as soon as we killed the lights for the night. I was always afraid for him. And then there was a guy whose girlfriend was taking lessons here and he waited for David one night and jumped him because David had taught the guy's girlfriend the pony. I mean, they didn't even touch or anything. David wasn't much of a fighter but my dad sure is. I screamed for him to come out and he really roughed up the guy pretty bad. Broke his nose and two of his fingers."

Chick Curtis came from the South Side of Chicago, back when a lot of it was still white. I'd seen him work over a guy in a tavern one night when the drunk had started ragging on Chick for being mobbed up. I don't think the whole encounter took a minute. Chick grabbed the drunk by the hair, slammed his forehead against the bar three or four times and then he stood him up straight and put one punch into the drunk's face and another to the guy's belly. There was blood everywhere. The guy was going to sue in civil court for damages, but then one of Chick's more sinister employees had a talk with him. No lawsuit was forthcoming.

"The bikers knew better. They only came around when my dad wasn't here." She frowned. "Then Rob Anderson and Nick Hannity used to come in. They'd pay for dance lessons and I'd lead one of them out to the floor but then they'd say, No, they wanted to dance with David. Really embarrass him like that. They thought it was really funny, of course. The people who were here to learn the dances really hated them. I was sort of afraid of what my dad would do to them if I ever told on them. But finally it got so bad with how they were picking on David that I didn't have any choice.

"He waited until they came in one night and then he took them out into the parking lot. I went out to try and stop him from really hurting them. There were a lot of their friends outside. They were all pretty drunk. My dad knew he'd get in trouble if he hurt them, so what he did was walk up to both of them and spit in their faces. Then he dared them to take the first swing. It was sort of funny because you know how short my dad is. Then he spit on them again. Their friends kept yelling for them to hit him. But they knew what would happen to them if they did. They finally just went away."

The door opened and a gentleman who had to be seventy-five walked in carefully. Glory jumped up and said, "Here, Mr. Winthrop, let me give you a hand."

"I'm gonna learn to mambo yet," the old man said and winked at me. "I'm taking the widow Harper to our class reunion and she says that's the only dance she likes."

Glory turned away from him momentarily and said to me, "I hope they find whoever killed him. I just wish they hadn't repealed the death penalty. I told Dad about David when he called in this morning and he said the same thing. He really liked David."

THE HOSPITAL WAS on the way back to my office, so I stopped in to inquire about the condition of my friend in the white Valiant. The one who liked to play in traffic.

"His condition is listed as fair," said the pleasant woman at the switchboard. She was the mother of one of my high school friends. She was legendary for her cheeseburgers, which she fixed every few weeks during the summer in the backyard whose lawn we all took turns mowing to keep her happy. "I'm afraid he can't have any visitors, Sam. Well, except for that new district attorney. She's up there now."

"She is?"

She smiled. "I can tell you've met her. She's a looker, isn't she?"

"Oh, she's all right if you like that much intelligence mixed with that much beauty."

"Same old Sam. You should settle down and get married like Bill did last year. She's already pregnant."

"How's he like St. Louis?"

"Oh, he's still adjusting. It's quite a change from our little town."

Jane Sykes was outside room 301 talking to a uniformed police officer.

No smile when she saw me approach. Just a barely perceptible nod. A yellow summer dress and a matching yellow straw hat. I was alive to other women and grateful to her for that. But I was also scared as hell, as I always was when I knew I'd already loosened my grip on the self-control handle.

When I reached her, she said, "So if you hear him even so much as mumble, be sure to get in there and try to catch what he's saying. Even if it doesn't make any sense."

"Sure, Miss Sykes." His eyes dazzled with fondness for the beautiful, stylish lady in front of him.

She didn't say anything to me, just nodded at the elevator. The doors were open, so we stepped inside.

"I know you can talk," I said, "I heard you just now telling that cop something."

"I'm saving it till we get to the cafeteria. I'm starving."

The typical hospital cafeteria. The nonmedical staffers sitting together enjoying leisurely lunches. The doctors and the nurses seeming in a bit more of a hurry.

Just once I'd like to play doctor. Walk around with a stethoscope dangling around my neck. In my high school days I'd been convinced that that was the easiest way of all to attract girls. While all the other boys were making fools of themselves trying to attract the most unattainable of girls, there I'd be walking up and down the ol' high school corridors, very cool in my white medical jacket and 'scope, a perfect combination of raw male sexuality and deep medical seriousness. Dr. Sam McCain, M.D.

She didn't order as if she were starving. Fruit cocktail, a bowl of chicken-rice soup, and a 7UP. I had a burger and a Pepsi.

"Now can we talk?"

"Sure."

"Have we found out his name yet?"

"'We' certainly have, Sam. James Neville."

"The same Neville as Richie Neville?"

"Half brother. They share a father."

"Any kind of record?"

"A long one. The biggest rap was for extortion. Served six years in Joliet. Armed robbery as a juvenile."

Will Neville, the man who blamed David Leeds for the murder of his brother, hadn't bothered to mention any James Neville. I'd have to talk to him again.

A doctor interrupted us. Young. Nice-looking. No

wedding ring. Leaning unnaturally close to Jane as he spoke. "I hope you got my invitation."

"I did, Dr. Higham. And I appreciate it."

"And even more, I hope you'll consider joining me."

"I'll get back to you."

He glanced at me and said, "I didn't know that DAs trafficked with defense attorneys."

Then she won my heart. "When they're as charming as Sam they do."

His smile was more of a grimace. Just the way I wanted it. He said good-bye and left.

"He made the mistake of pawing me at the party Judge Martin gave for me. Very possessive. Not the right approach, not for me anyway."

"Me, either. I hate to be pawed."

"Very funny, McCain. Now tell me what you're going to do about Neville upstairs?"

"About Neville upstairs I plan to see his slug of a brother. And then I plan to find this biker." I told her what I'd heard in the barbershop.

"Now that's interesting, if it's true."

Not until then, me being a slow learner, especially when I'm so taken with a woman, did I realize what was happening here.

"We're working together."

"Yes, we are, Sam. And that's just the way I planned it. I confide in you, you confide in me. Neither Clifford nor Judge Whitney has to know. The point is to serve justice, as stuffy as that sounds."

"This is like a secret club."

She smiled, shaking her head. "Here's my unlisted number at home. You'd better write it down."

Then she went and spoiled our little movie moment. "And please don't call me at this number unless it's business. I need my private time, Sam."

"Yeah, me too," I said, though that's all I'd had since Mary had gone back to Wes. Private time.

I NEEDED MORE information about James Neville. It was likely he was staying in one of the local hotels, maybe even the one my old friend Dink worked at. I called his home.

"Dink, please."

"He isn't here right now."

"Please, Mrs. Dink—"

"Are you trying to be funny?"

"You don't recognize my voice?"

"The TV's up too loud."

"Look, I know he's there because you won't let him go out unless he's going to work."

"He tell you that?"

"It was my idea."

"Oh, then this is McCain."

"Yes."

"Darn right he don't go out. He only gets in trouble." I didn't tell her that I was calling to get him in some trouble for me.

"Well, I wonder if I could talk to him."

"They didn't cancel his bail, did they?"

"No, but I need him to do me a favor."

Suspicious. "What kind of a favor?"

"He's still at the hotel every day?"

"Yeah, his uncle's the only one who'd hire him."

"Good. Then I need to talk to him."

"I don't want him in no more trouble."

The way I had figured it out, he wouldn't have to get in any trouble if he did what I told him.

"He'll be fine."

"And I didn't appreciate that 'Mrs. Dink.'"

"I apologize."

"I'll go get him."

When he came on the line, Dink said, "The wife, she don't care for you much."

"I called her Mrs. Dink."

"That ain't why. She said you shoulda got me off on probation."

"I *did* get you off on probation. Then you stole that cop's billfold. That's why you're headed back to court."

"Oh, yeah, I guess she forgot that."

"Listen to me. I need you to do something for me."

He listened.

"Thanks, McCain." He lowered his voice. "I've been needin' to do something illegal. I'm goin' nuts here."

"It's not illegal. Not if you do it the way I told you."

"Well, at least it's sneaky. That's a start in the right direction."

"Remember what you need to do, now."

"You knock something off on the bill?"

"You mean the bill neither you nor your parents have paid me anything on for five years?"

"I guess you got a point there."

"Call me as soon as you do it."

THIRTEEN

I DROVE PAST both of the garages where the bikers tended to hang out when they weren't at the Iron Cross, the tavern on the edge of town where the local gendarmes had to come in full force several times a week to break up fights. The local gendarmes often looked worse than the bikers when it was all done.

But there were no signs of Harleys or Indians anywhere. I assumed they were out on the highway or at one of their enclaves in the nearby woods.

I found a Debbie Todd Carlyle in the phone book and drove on out to the hardscrabble little acreage where chickens seemed to have taken over. They were everywhere. I had to park on the edge of the gravel road. There were too many of them in the drive to scatter.

Debbie, a heavyset woman in a red-and-black checked flannel shirt and jeans, stood with her hands on her hips watching me approach. She didn't look happy.

When I had to slow down because I was entangled in chickens, she said, "You might as well go back to town, McCain. I don't plan to talk to you."

"I just came out to buy some chickens."

"You know where you can shove your chickens."

"Any special reason you seem to hate me? Your sister and I were good friends."

"Good friends, my ass. She'd still be alive if it wasn't for you. She shoulda kept her nose out of it."

I was marooned on the front lawn amidst a sea of gabby white chickens. The one-story house in front of me needed a coat of paint and the 1949 Pontiac up on blocks needed a left front door.

"She was murdered."

"You think I don't know that, McCain? That's exactly what I told her would happen, butting in like that."

They pecked, they squawked, they shat. Their heads jerked back and forth. They were pretty ugly creatures when you came right down to it. But you had to feel sorry for them. They had but one mission on this planet. To be consumed.

I worked myself through a clutch of them, drawing a few feet closer to the small, old house.

"If you know she was murdered, Debbie, you should want to help me."

"And end up like she did?"

"Did she tell you what she saw?"

"No, she didn't. I told her not to. I didn't want to get caught up in all this crap." She had a broad face that would have been attractive if she'd wanted to make it so with a little soap and makeup. But she was a widow—her husband had died in a freak accident with a combine—and a doggedly antisocial one at that.

"So you might as well get out of here, McCain. I don't know nothing about what she saw or didn't see. That's between you and her."

"She's dead, Debbie. You're the only one who can help me." Then: "She saw something, Debbie. Something to do with the murders the other night. You were her best friend. She must have told you something."

"I said that she didn't, McCain. Now I'm going back inside and finish my lunch."

And that was all. She turned, went back inside, and closed and locked the door behind her.

And left me with the chickens. Their squawks were putting me on edge. "How about keeping it down?" I said.

Which, of course, did me a lot of good. If anything, they seemed suddenly louder.

They trailed me back to my ragtop. A pied piper I was. I got in my car and started up the engine. I decided to go up to the far end of the road and take the blacktop back to town. Shorter route and less damage to the machine than on this scaly road.

I roared the mufflers three or four times. The chickens scattered. I didn't want to grind one of them to death beneath my wheels.

I set off, turning up the radio as I did so. The local stations still played Elvis's "Return to Sender" from last year. I liked hearing Elvis sing just about anything, though I already missed his original sound when he was with Sun Records and covering songs like "Milk Cow Boogie" and "Blue Moon of Kentucky." Hard to grow up out here without at least a sneaking fondness for real country music.

Also hard to grow up out here without a real desire to protect your blood kin. People like Debbie always bothered me. I just didn't understand how you could write off a sister the way she had.

FOURTEEN

"I WOULDN'T GO IN there if I was you."

"It's a public place, isn't it?"

"Not really. Especially not to fuzz."

"Technically, I'm not fuzz. I'm private."

"Yeah, but you work for the judge. You know how many Devils she's sent up?"

"Two, that I remember."

"Well, you remember wrong. Four. And two of 'em are still doin' time."

The Iron Cross was a one-story concrete-block building that had been painted black, apparently to suit the mood of the bikers who drank there. At this hour of the day the front and sides of the place were packed with motorcycles. The jukebox inside trembled with gut-bucket rock and roll. And the laughter was of the coarse, ugly kind of pirates in all those buried-treasure movies.

The man I was talking to was named Ray Peters. He was a sort of honorary biker. He'd lost a leg and an arm in Korea and now got around on a single crutch. The word his brother gave me—his brother being a nonbiker who ran illegal crap games and was frequently in need of my legal services—was that Ray never felt right around "normal" people. So he dressed in a sleeveless denim jacket, jeans tucked into motorcycle boots, and an eyepatch he justified wearing by saying that his left eye had been damaged in Korea, too. He had one big problem that I could see. Take away the rebellion and what you had was a sad, lonely, and very decent guy.

"How about I do you a favor?" he said, as if to prove my point. His blond-gray hair was so thin on top the sun had already baked his scalp brick red.

"A favor?"

"You tell me who you want to see and I'll go in and get him and see if he'll come out."

"Won't that get you in trouble?"

A bleak smile. "Nah. They don't pick on gimps till real late at night."

"Nice folks."

"They don't pity me, anyway, McCain. And they don't make fun of me. You take your nice, normal people—they wouldn't let me fit in even if I wanted to."

Even if some of that was paranoia, I knew how he felt. Or should I say I presumed to know how he felt? Being short and coming from the Knolls had made me into an outsider of sorts, too. But I was strictly a tourist. There was a French saying I'd picked up from a Graham Greene novel—"Embrace your fate." I was pretty sure mine was a whole lot easier to embrace than poor Ray's. He had to live his out every second of every moment when another human eye was on him.

"So who is it you want to see?"

"De Ruse."

He laughed. "Man, you picked just about the meanest son of a bitch in the whole wolf pack. De Ruse. You sure you want to talk to him?"

"Yeah."

"You packin'?"

"I've got my old .45 in the glove compartment."

"Maybe you should transfer it to your coat. One of the guys who's still servin' time is his brother."

"Good thing I'm a mean son of a bitch myself, huh?"

He laughed again. "I don't know about mean. Crazy might be closer."

He adjusted his crutch and said, "You sure?"

"I'm sure."

When the door opened, a hurricane of dank smells violated the soft, sunny afternoon. Smoke, beer, whiskey, marijuana, and a toilet that the UN might cite as a weapon of mass destruction.

De Ruse came right out.

The muscles in his arms rippled like crawling snakes.

His green eyes gleamed with enormous malice.

He was alone.

He didn't need anybody else.

He was strutting.

With his big loop earring and his bare chest and his red Indian-style bandana around his blond head, he looked like somebody who'd give Spiderman a whole raft of shit, Spidey being the only comic book I still read.

He threw the right hand from at least a foot and a half away. Given his short legs, just throwing it should have knocked him off balance. It didn't. And traveling such a distance, and it being only one punch, its power should have been cut at least in half. It wasn't.

There was quick, sharp, overwhelming pain, and then there was nothing.

I woke up sometime later with my wrists bound up

in the necktie I'd been wearing and the rest of the tie wrapped around the rear bumper of my ragtop.

De Ruse was dragging me around the dusty lot of the Iron Cross to the great and abiding amusement of maybe twenty Road Devils.

The Road Devilettes, or whatever you called them, laughed especially hard. I knew right then and there that I probably wasn't ever going to sleep with any of them, much as that was to be desired, with their beehive hairdos and witches'-brew cackles.

The point wasn't to hurt me, it was to humiliate me. The soil was loose and sandy and he probably wasn't even going fifteen miles an hour. The big fear was pieces of glass scattered across the lot, but the worst I got was the occasional scrape from small rocks. He was being careful without seeming to understand that simply by knocking me out he was already in trouble and probably on his way back to the state pen.

He went in wide circles. I didn't try to get loose. That would give them too much pleasure.

He drove close enough to them so that they could spit on me, which they took the opportunity to do. But at least they didn't hit my face. I imagined that my trousers and jacket were beyond even the healing powers of dry cleaning.

And then he decided to give me a little scare. He floored it. We tore across a long sandy patch that ended up near a creek at maybe forty miles an hour. Now there was pain.

Behind us the Devils were shouting and applauding. And then it was over.

He shut off the ignition and shouted "Beers're on me!" and then ran back to the crowd.

This was how the truly cool guy would handle himself. He had not given me any formal verbal recognition. He'd hit me, he'd dragged me around. But he hadn't acknowledged me as a person in any other way.

And he still hadn't.

They hailed their hero and then went back into the tavern, thunder of jukebox, unholy stench of toilet.

Leaving me to start the process of getting to my feet and untying myself. It didn't take long and it wasn't difficult. Restoring my dignity would be another matter altogether.

I was in the process of taking off my loafers and dumping the sand out when I heard the tavern door open. But I was already prepared for a return match.

Ray crutched his way over to me. "You all right?"

"All right? A tough guy like me?"

We both smiled at that one.

"He can be a real asshole sometimes."

"I find that hard to believe, Ray. Seemed like a real nice fella to me."

He moved a few feet closer for a better look at me. "No offense, but you sound kinda crazy."

And I suppose I was. In a business like mine, whether I'm investigating for myself or the judge, you meet people who do their best to belittle you any way they can. I used to be able to deal with it. But as I got older I got tired of insults, innuendos, jibes. And when I got tired enough, I'd push back. These were almost always verbal battles.

But being punched out and dragged across a parking

lot for the entertainment of a bunch of bikers—that was a special kind of debasement.

What I should've done was find a phone and call out the gendarmes to arrest him. And that had been my first impulse. But then I remembered that not only had I been humiliated, I hadn't even done my job, which was to ask him about being spotted at the murder scene the other night.

Ray said, "Some of them're afraid he'll get sent back to prison."

"Aw, that'd be too bad now, wouldn't it?"

"They said to tell you he was only havin' some fun was all."

"A growing boy needs to have some fun, doesn't he?" And right then I knew that I did sound crazy. That in my voice you could hear rage and tears that I couldn't control. "I'll tell you what, Ray. You go back in there and tell him to come out here by himself and we'll talk."

"You mean you might not get him sent up again?"

"We'll see how it goes. Now you go back in there and tell him."

He was still studying my face. He was still sensing how near being unhinged I was.

"Well, I'll go tell him."

"By himself, remember. And nobody else is to come out until I open the door. You got that?"

"I'm sorry this happened, Mr. McCain. I truly am."

He stared at me a little more and then started working his pained way back to the tavern.

I flipped the trunk open, got what I needed, and when he went inside, positioned myself next to the door.

I knew I wouldn't have much time. There was a back door, and a few of them would undoubtedly sneak out to back him up.

Like the good thug he was, he let some time go by. Get me nervous, uncertain, so he'd have the advantage when he strode through the door.

But I was neither nervous nor uncertain. I was crazy pissed is what I was.

And so when he was less than four feet from the door closing behind him, I moved.

He'd been looking straight ahead for me. By the time he decided to look to his left, I was bringing the tire iron down on the side of his head.

He did a cartoon take. He staggered backwards but for a second there he looked as if he was going to shrug it off, the way those professional wrestlers do after the opponent hits them with a chair.

He even gave me a little professional wrestler grin. But then blood bloomed on the spot where I'd hit him and his eyes got hazy and he collapsed. Just hit the ground in a pile of unwashed flesh, tattoos, and now free-flowing blood.

I just had time to drag him over to my ragtop before three of his buddies came running along the side of the building.

But they were too late. I had my .45 jammed into his face. He was still unconscious, sitting on the ground with his back to my passenger door.

"You boys go back inside. This is between us. If you stay inside for fifteen minutes, I won't file any charges. I won't even mention it to his parole officer. But if I see anybody before the fifteen minutes is up, I'll have the cops out here and they'll bust every one of you. Now get back inside."

They had to sneer and threaten and make a show of it. But they knew they didn't have any choice. One of them, the one most likely to have studied under Gandhi, flipped me the bird just before he disappeared into the stench inside.

It hadn't taken much to calm me down. I'd hit him hard enough to draw blood and the sight of that blood was enough to pacify me.

As he came back to Planet Earth, I said, "Now I want you to tell me what you were doing out at Neville's the other night."

"Go to hell."

Then I learned that I wasn't quite as pacified as I'd thought. This time I pistol-slapped him right across the face and broke his nose. I hadn't intended to, but fortune of war and all that.

He started crying. Not from the pain, I was pretty sure. But from the humiliation. He would have to go back inside and explain to them how somebody who weighed less than his left arm had knocked him out and then busted his nose.

"You're gonna pay for this, McCain. You mother—"

And then I grabbed his hair and gave it a twist and raised him an inch or two from the ground. "Why were you out at Neville's the other night?"

"I wasn't! I wasn't there!"

Screeching his words now. A good sign.

I gave his greasy hair another twist and then slammed his head against the door.

And then he collapsed. Emotionally. I let go of his hair. His head slumped. The blood was running faster and thicker from his head. He was snuffling up air through his busted nose. Crying and choking sometimes.

"You tell me the truth, I won't press charges against you. And I mean the truth right now."

"You bastard," he said through the phlegm and blood.

"That's not a good start. You want to try again?"

I was just about to step on his hand—sadism is a lot more fun than it sounds—when he said, "The pictures."

"The what?"

"The pictures. The photographs."

"What photographs?"

"That we paid Neville to take of Phelps."

"Phelps the cop?"

"Yeah."

His nose was getting bloodier. I dug in my back pocket and pulled out my handkerchief. Tossed it on his lap. "Christmas came early."

I gave him a few minutes to do what he could with the handkerchief. "This really hurts, man."

I wondered how many innocents had said that to him over the years after he pounded on them.

"What about Phelps?"

"He busted Charlie Eagle for grass."

"Yeah, I heard about that. So what? He was just doing his job."

"Bullshit, he was doing his job, man. He caught two of us smoking grass one night sittin' on our bikes downtown and you know what he did? Took our grass and smoked it himself. Never charged us."

He tried to shake his head but misery cragged his face instantly. "We knew Phelps was seein' this Mexican chick over by the rail yards. Her old man is a switch-man, works nights. We had Neville take some pictures of Phelps goin' in the door at her place. We were gonna use them against Phelps, see if he'd tell the DA that maybe he made a mistake, you know, with Charlie Eagle."

I was amazed at his ignorance. "The trial's already been scheduled. If Phelps backed out now, the DA would know that somebody got to him."

He angled his head up. Between the blood and the bruises he was one sorry biker.

"So that's why I was at Neville's, but him and that colored boy were dead when I got there."

"You find the pictures?"

"Too scared, man. Somebody sees me there, they'll nail me for them bein' dead for sure." He snorted. "I knew somebody'd get to Neville someday."

"Why?"

"Why? He took pictures of people all the time. Secret shit, I mean. He'd hang out in different spots at night and see things and hear things and then he'd start fol-lowing somebody, see if the rumors was true. And if they was, he'd start takin' pictures."

Good old Neville. I'd congratulated myself on him staying out of trouble, thinking that he'd learned his lesson just the way young men do every night on TV. Crime Doesn't Pay and all that. Maybe burglary or car theft or armed robbery didn't pay because you could get caught so easily.

But blackmail was a more subtle crime, one infinitely more difficult to prove—because the blackmail-ee had a vested interest in protecting the blackmailer.

"And that's the truth, man. Everything I just said. Now, was you telling the truth, McCain? About not tellin' my parole officer?"

"Far as I'm concerned, we're even up."

"I got the worst of it."

"Good." I didn't smile. "Now get your ass up. I want to get out of here."

"Good thing you work for the judge, McCain. Otherwise I'd get up right now and beat your ass bloody."

"Jeez, man, and here I thought we were friends."

I STOPPED BY my office to see if any money had come in. My body was a universe of pain, large and small. While I was going through the mail, Dink called.

He said, "It wasn't as much fun as I figured it would be."

"Well, I'm sorry you didn't get to commit a felony, Dink."

"I got to work early just like you told me so I could get one of the maids to let me in his room, see—"

That had been my plan. Get Dink into James Neville's room and see what he could find.

"But you know what?"

"What?"

"I didn't even have to find a maid to con into it."

"No?"

"Rosemary—the one with the lazy eye?—she was in there when I got there."

"Good old Rosemary. So what did you find?"

"He's got a lot of dirty magazines."

"Uh-huh."

"And a lot of socks. He must have twenty pairs."

"Good for him."

"I know the kind of thing you wanted me to find. And I only found one thing. It's this brochure."

"Brochure?"

"Yeah. It's pretty chintzy-lookin'. It's for a photography studio. The Neville Brothers Studio, it says."

It had been well worth the trip. "Dink, that's great."

"I wanted to steal it—you know, I wanted to get a *little* something out of it. But then I remembered you said only go in when a maid lets you in and don't take nothin' out of it."

"I appreciate it, Dink."

"The wife thinks I'm goin' to prison."

"I'll do my best for you, Dink. I just wish we didn't have to go up against the same judge."

He paused. "Listen, anytime you want me to sneak in someplace for you, just give me a call. I don't think you appreciate the full range of my talents yet, McCain."

Lord God Almighty.

"I'm sure I don't, Dink. I'm sure I don't."

FIFTEEN

THANKS TO THE NEW procedures that Jane Sykes had forced Cliffie to follow, the entire area around Neville's cabin was now set off as a crime scene. Nobody was allowed past the sawhorses that formed a square around the area.

The day was closing as I got out of my ragtop. The birdsong and the long shadows and the purpling clouds were as lonesome as a Hank Williams song. I brought along the outsized flashlight I'd bought a year ago at Western Auto.

I started inside the cabin. The darkroom looked even worse than it had the night of the murders, everything busted up in a frantic search. And now I knew for what.

The whole idea of blackmail had a big-city feel to it. Every other episode of *Perry Mason* used it as a device and every once in a while the *Chicago Trib* would run a crime story that involved it, though it was usually described as extortion.

I worked till near dark. I pretty much knew I wouldn't find anything. Richie Neville had been a smart young man. The sort of crime he was committing meant that he had to be careful where he hid the photographs he used. And that meant that he probably didn't leave them in his cabin. But it had to be checked.

Weariness from being dragged all over the parking lot had begun to sneak up on me. I needed a drink and a shower, and then a meal.

I was just leaving the cabin when I saw a stack of business envelopes on an overstuffed chair, one of the few pieces not to be knocked over. My first thought was that one of the police officers had probably gone through the envelopes. But then I remembered Cliffie was in charge. I sat down with my flashlight and went to work and came away with one interesting fact. I extricated a monthly statement from one of the six bank envelopes and got back to my ragtop.

THE MEAL TURNED OUT to be a fried egg sandwich, a glass of V8, and a slice of birthday cake I'd brought home about a week ago and kept in the refrigerator.

I kept wanting to give Jane Sykes a call. Officially, I had business to discuss with her. Unofficially, I just wanted to hear her laugh. I enjoyed sitting in my apartment with the cats all over me, watching an inane situation comedy and not thinking about Mary and would she ever change her mind and come back to me.

I was thinking about Jane Sykes and wondering if there was any kind of future there.

The shower had been nice—I had a lot more bruises than I'd realized from the dragging—but it hadn't revived me. Sitting there in my boxers with the cats, I was starting to give in to sleep.

In fact, I was dozing when the phone rang.

Good news—possibly Mary or Jane calling.

Bad news—my dad had had another heart attack.

All these thoughts before I was truly awake. Automatic thoughts.

"Hello."

"Did I wake you up?"

"No, uh-uh, I was just going over some work."

"Gee, I hope I get you on the witness stand sometime. You're a terrible liar. You'd be so easy to break."

"Thank you for that and all the other compliments."

"I heard a rumor you had kind of a rough time this afternoon."

"That's all it is, Jane. A rumor."

"So you don't want anything legal done about it?"

"Not so far. Let's wait and see what happens."

With my usual grace I quickly changed the subject.

"What's the word from the hospital on James Neville?"

"No change. Still unconscious." Then: "Are those cats in the background?"

"Yes, and cruelly mistreated cats. They haven't been fed for upwards of twenty minutes."

I could hear the smile in her voice. "My little kitten died when she was only six months old. I'm afraid to get another one. I don't want to go through that heartbreak again. You should've seen her. Gray fur and these sweet little white paws."

"For a DA, you really have a sentimental side."

"Whatever you do, don't tell anybody about it." Then: "Well, I'll talk to you tomorrow. 'Night, Sam."

"'Night."

After we hung up, I stood in the light of the refrigerator eating what remained of that large chunk of cake.

I also finished off the beer I'd started as soon as I'd gotten in. I'm not sure you'll find that particular combination—cake and beer, in your average cookbook, but it's not as bad as you'd think.

The phone again.

No doubt it was Jane asking me to spend the night with her. Or Mary saying that she'd made a very bad mistake and was coming back to me. Or Janet Leigh asking me if I'd mind taking a shower with her because she was still scared after *Psycho*.

The voice was male and tainted with whiskey.

"This phone may be tapped, so listen to me. I'll be sitting on a bench by the wading pool at six a.m. tomorrow morning. I expect to see you there, too."

A teasing familiarity, that voice. But he hadn't spoken long enough for me to identify it.

A RESTLESS NIGHT. Not just because of the late call but also because I was beginning to think that Richie Neville hadn't been alone in his blackmail operation. His brother James probably hadn't come to town just to say hello. With his record for extortion, he had most likely played a part in the whole scheme.

And there was another reason for my restlessness. The bank statement indicated that four months ago Richie Neville had paid a year in advance for a safe-deposit box. I was eager to get in there and see. I'd need the permission of either Judge Whitney or Jane Sykes, but I was sure that one of them would grant it.

The one aspect of the murders I'd yet to piece together was the relationship of Richie Neville and David Leeds. Why had Leeds been at the cabin? What had he wanted with Neville? Given what I could reasonably surmise, Richie possessed far more salacious photos of Lucy and David than had been sent to the party office. The senator would have no choice but to pay a good deal of money for them.

The final thought was one I didn't want to have in my head, but I had to consider it at least. Were Richie and David working together? Was David helping Richie get some especially good photos for the camera?

I hoped not. I just kept seeing Marie Leeds's face as we talked and sat in the booth at Woolworth's. Grief enough that her brother had been murdered, intolerable that he'd been part of the scheme that had likely caused all the violence.

The cats, sprawled across various points of my bed, got a lot more sleep than I did.

SIXTEEN

HE WASN'T THERE.

I'd taken a cold shower, gunned three cups of steaming coffee, and chain-smoked half a dozen cigarettes just so I could be awake when I met him.

And he wasn't there.

The summer morning almost made up for it. The birds sounded happy as drunks at a party and the clouds were as white as they'd been in those great old Technicolor pirate movies. The dew-gleaming grass had a sweet, almost narcotic aroma and the breeze reminded me of my brother Robert, long dead now, and how we'd always flown kites on such mornings as this.

I could almost forget how much our town was changing. Chain stores and chain burger joints and chain supermarkets starting to push our own merchants out. And the bedroom commuters a community unto themselves, separate and superior.

And then, behind the bench where I was sitting, a voice said: "Back here, McCain."

He was hiding behind the god-awful pink concession stand that in summer bloomed with moms and kids and the smell of hot dogs.

His head was all I could see, and even that I didn't see much of, given how low the brim was snapped on his fedora and the large sunglasses that made identification even tougher.

"Back here."

I walked back.

When I was within ten feet of him, I knew who he was. And given who he was, I guessed he was probably right holding a meeting the way spies did in the James Bond novels.

"I'm sorry for all this," Senator Lloyd Williams said.

He made no move to take off the hat or the shades.

We were screened by a dense run of pine trees behind us. Safe.

"My opponent hires operatives to follow me around."

"Of course you'd never do anything like that."

"I do it only because the other side does it."

"Of course."

"You always were a sarcastic bastard."

"Are we here to run each other down, Senator, because if we are, I want to remind you what a chickenshit you were in sticking up for Senator McCarthy. Not to mention all the bullshit laws you've introduced to hurt poor people."

I'd forgotten what a cranky bastard I could be in the morning when somebody irritated me.

"I can see I've made a mistake."

He turned to go, the long body buried in a long tan trench coat whose collar ran all the way up under the back of his hat.

"Look, Senator, you got me out of bed this early, so I deserve at least the courtesy of an explanation."

He turned back toward me. "You don't like me and

I don't like you. That's hardly the basis for a good working relationship."

I'm rarely shocked these days. I was shocked. "You want to hire me?"

He was silent for a time. Those big, dark plastic bug eyes staring at me. "I wanted to hire you because I believe you're as good as your word."

"I like to think I am. I try to be. Sometimes things go wrong, of course. Beyond my control."

"But you wouldn't blackmail me. You'd do the job I hired you to do and that would be that."

"You're talking about Richie Neville."

"Yes."

"And him having photos of David Leeds and your daughter."

"No."

This time I think I actually flinched when he answered me.

No? Not his white daughter going out with a black man? What else would he hire me for?

"We need to make a deal right now. Before you say anything more."

He nodded. "All right. I do want to hire you, then. But given your situation with the judge, can I be assured that you won't share any information you gather with anybody else?"

"I'll give you my word as long as the information I gather doesn't cover up a crime."

"Not a crime—a stupid—" He touched long fingers to his cheek. "I'm so exhausted from worrying about this that I can't even think clearly." Then: "Indiscretion. A stupid indiscretion." Then: "A local woman. A promi-

nent woman. Her brother has a fishing cabin. A very
nice one. He's been in Europe for the past few years.
That's where we—she and I—got together. And that's
where Richie Neville took photographs of us."

"Marsha Lane."

"My God, how did you know?"

"Prominent woman. Brother in Europe. Nice fishing
cabin. You forget I work downtown. Had to be Marsha
Lane." Then: "I can see what you're up against. First
Lucy and David Leeds. And now Marsha Lane. Your
campaign's going to be a nightmare."

He leaned back against the concession stand. He
took out a pack of Chesterfields and lighted one with a
Zippo. He hadn't relaxed; he'd damned near collapsed.
Even his voice was weaker. "I've thought of announc-
ing that I wasn't going to run again. But my family—
if I announced that, the press would be all over. They'd
know I was hiding something." Then: "Ironically, I
think I can weather Lucy and her young gentleman.
But with Marsha added to it—" He threw his cigarette
away. "It's funny you're the only one I can trust. But
who knows what you're getting when you hire one of
those Chicago agencies. They could be just as mercen-
ary as Neville." Then: "What a great fix this is, huh?
Somebody like you is my only hope."

I didn't like him. He brought out all my class anger.
He'd been an overindulged preppy who'd come back
here summers to tell everybody of his manly conquests
back East. He'd never carried this county because so
many people in their forties remembered him all too
well.

But what he was talking about was a principle.

Whatever I thought of him, he didn't deserve to be blackmailed.

"I'll tell you what, Senator. I won't make any kind of deal with you except to say that whatever I find, I'll turn over to you. I want to see you defeated but not because of some pictures. You don't pay me anything, I don't tell anybody about this, and whatever I find is yours."

"I'm sorry I shot off my mouth and called you a name."

My laugh was harsh. "That was a moment of truth, Senator. We basically hate each other. And a moment of truth coming from a politician is something to be happy about."

I started to turn away from him. "I'll be in touch."

"Can't I at least say thank you?"

This time I was the one who regretted being a bit nasty. I turned back to him and stuck out my hand. We shook.

"Thanks, McCain."

I walked back to my ragtop.

SEVENTEEN

DEAR MR SSAMPSON
Please remit your bill, which is attached. This is
the third time we've have sent it.
Sincerely,

Then, in light pencil: Needs your cig here, Mr. C.

"Cig" meaning signature.

"Think you could run this through the typewriter
one more time, Jamie?"

"Was there something wrong with it?"

"Just a few things."

"I really took my time with that one, too, Mr. C."

"I just made little marks on it."

I placed it on the edge of my desk for her to pick up.
She wore a tight mauve blouse and a short tan skirt. She
also smelled great. In the face of such things, what are
a few typos?

The phone rang. I grabbed it.

No greetings and salutations. "Since you're on
salary, would it be too much to ask that you stop by my
office?"

"I'd be honored to."

"And I mean now."

"Delighted to. Five minutes?"

"How about three? You're not that far away."

Just as I hung up, the mailman came through the door. His name was Henry Woolsey and he was an unabashed admirer of Jamie's, fifty-some years notwithstanding.

"'Morning, Jamie."

"'Morning, Henry. I see you broke out your shorts already."

"Plenty warm for them. Too bad Sam won't let you wear shorts."

"Why don't I just let her wear one of those French bikinis, Henry? Would that be good enough for you?"

Henry's furiously flushed face contrasted vividly with his white hair.

"He's always kidding around like that, Henry," Jamie said. "He wouldn't actually let me wear anything like that to the office."

Henry started dealing out the pieces of mail as if they were cards and we were playing poker. I immediately saw what all the envelopes had in common. She just looked so innocent poised on the edge of her chair, I had to say it gently: "Gee, I guess I must have forgotten to put stamps on all these envelopes last night. Would you do that for me, Jamie?"

I was already late for the judge. Three minutes can go by awfully fast.

"I'll probably be back in an hour or so," I said.

Henry, the lecher, was already helping himself to the coffee. Young women like Jamie were in need of protection, no doubt, and Henry was only too eager to lend a hand.

He winked at me. "I like that idea you have for a French bikini, Sam."

AFTER I BROUGHT HER up to date, she said, "My spies tell me you spent some time with Jane Sykes."

"True enough. Your spies got something right for once."

Judge Esme Anne Whitney's office was one of timeless solemnity: deep leather chairs, rich carpeting, flawless wainscoting, two full walls of legal tomes, and a desk big enough to play a passing fair game of Ping-Pong on. It was always cleared off.

"Maybe you haven't noticed, McCain, but the Sykes family is our enemy. They stand for everything we revile—or at least that I revile. And I assumed you did, too."

"She's cleaning up the police force, for one thing. And for another, she's not going along with all of Cliffie's arrests."

"And she's very good-looking."

"Really? I hadn't noticed that."

"I don't want you to see her anymore."

Per usual, she parked herself on the edge of the desk with a Gauloise and a cup of coffee laced with brandy. No rubber bands this morning, which was an indicator of how seriously she took this.

"I'm serious, McCain."

She looked regal in her fitted gray dress and over-sized, vaguely African-style earrings. No wonder she'd managed to find four men to marry her. Even in her sixties, she was still a desirable woman, if, that is, you caught her before a day's worth of sipping brandy-soaked coffee began to take its toll.

"You can order me not to work with her. That comes under the heading of employment. But you can't order me not to see her for pleasure. That comes under the heading of private life."

This was my morning for shocks as she said, "I thought we were friends, McCain."

My instinct was to laugh. The words hadn't come out right, which I'd put down to bad acting. But then I saw the shimmer of tears in her ice-blue eyes and knew better.

The judge had never before said anything like this to me. She'd always made it clear that she'd hired me because she couldn't find anybody any better who lived here in town. Not exactly your ringing endorsement. Never warm, most of the time barely courteous, sometimes damned mean, she was fond of reminding me of her social background and position and my lack thereof.

And now this. Served with tears yet. But those first tears were now followed by more tears that actually escaped her eyes and sparkled on her cheeks.

"I just feel so damned alone sometimes, McCain. No friends to confide in except back East; nobody to have dinner with at the end of the day."

I knew what I was seeing, of course, but now wasn't the time to talk about it. In the years I'd been her court investigator, I'd seen her drinking get increasingly serious. And now she was at the point where she needed to make the trip up to the Minnesota clinic that was disguised as a resort for rich people.

Four, even two years ago, she would never have let me see her so vulnerable. She enjoyed being imperious. She even enjoyed jokes about being imperious.

I found myself standing up and walking to her. I found myself putting my hands gently on her shoulders.

And she found herself jerking away from me and snapping, "Don't you dare ever touch me like that, McCain! I'm your employer, not one of your little strumpets!"

I thought of explaining myself but realized it wouldn't help either of us. I'd embarrassed her. I'd damaged her pride. People just didn't go around touching imperious people the way they would little strumpets.

There was only one thing left for me to do. I walked to the door. "I'll give you my word that I will never cooperate with Jane Sykes on a case. If we have a relationship, it'll be strictly a personal one. And if that's not good enough, then—"

"Just get the hell out of here, McCain, and don't come around until I tell you to."

She was drinking deeply from her cup as I quietly closed the door and stepped out into the hallway.

WALTER MARGOLIN HAD BEEN a particularly obnoxious hall monitor. We'd always had the sense that he was too goody-goody even for the nuns. I remember Sister Mary Rosemary standing behind him while he was ragging on some poor little girl for taking too long at the water fountain. The sister rolled her eyes as Walter became more and more dramatic.

In his graying crew cut, huge red bow tie, and tan summer-weight suit with enough patriotic pins on it to start a war, Walter was now a grown-up version of a hall monitor.

He was vice president of loans at First Trust Bank. His desk sat in front of the vault, and it was to him that supplicants came to plead their cases. I'd always thought he should have a kneeler in front of his desk, the way you do in confessionals. Because from what I'd been told, you had to show Walter a great deal of deference and piety before he would even consider your loan.

He looked up and gave me the hall monitor's smirk he'd perfected by the time we were in fourth grade.

"Well, well, well, I knew you'd be in here someday, McCain. Destitute and in dire need of help." The smirk got smirkier. "Do you remember seventh grade?"

"Barely. I was drunk for most of it."

"Very funny, McCain. I seem to remember a certain juvenile delinquent who dropped a water balloon on my head from the third floor."

"I was framed, Walter."

"And now," he said with great satisfaction, leaning back in his executive chair, "you've come here to see if I'll be decent enough to forget how you humiliated me and give you a loan."

I tossed the envelope on his desk. "That's court permission to open Richie Neville's safe-deposit box."

He leaned forward. "That's not going to happen. Only the person designated as his closest family member can open that now."

"Open it up and read it."

"You don't seem to understand, McCain—but then you were never real bright, anyway—that court orders don't matter. We have our own rules of procedure here."

"If you say so, Walter."

I snatched back the envelope and headed straight for the large corner office where the bank president resided when he wasn't attending vital banking conferences in the Bahamas or playing nine rounds at the country club.

I got what I wanted.

"Here, Sam, let me take care of that for you. We can open that safe-deposit box right now."

There was a tremor in his voice that attracted a few glances and he came upon me so fast he almost bumped into me.

But he did lead me to the large solemn room in which the safe-deposit boxes were kept.

THERE WAS MORE THAN three thousand dollars in cash and four manila envelopes with familiar last names written in ink on them. I took a quick glance inside and found photographic negatives. I didn't look at any of them.

THE NEW BLACK CADILLAC didn't belong in one of the three parking slots that came with my office. Neither did the man sitting behind the wheel.

He got out of his car as soon as I got out of mine.

"I suppose you'll grow up someday, Sam, and get an adult car instead of that convertible."

"And I suppose you'll grow up someday, Anderson, and stop bleeding poor people dry."

"Nobody else will loan them money. I have to charge the rates I do. And I don't intend to defend myself to somebody like you."

"You just did. Now what the hell do you want?"

"I want you to leave my son alone. Because if you don't, you'll be damned sorry."

Rob Anderson's father was tall, slim, sour, and a professional nag. He owned four loan companies throughout the state that were the last resort for debt-ridden people. I'd seen it calculated that his loan rate ended up being in the fifty-five percent area by the time a loan was paid off. The money he made, and it was as much as anybody made in our town, automatically made him respectable, never mind that he traded on human misery. He was an elder in his Lutheran church, he frequently wrote guest editorials for the newspaper, and he even ran radio spots that were long enough to promote his usurious business and give him forty-five seconds to expound on how America was in the process of losing its moral compass. Whatever the hell that was. He was one of the Midwest grotesques Sherwood Anderson and Sinclair Lewis had identified as sui generis long, long ago.

"I haven't been bothering him, but the police probably have."

"Uh-huh. And who put it in their minds that he had anything to do with that damned colored boy?"

"I didn't have to put anything in their minds, Anderson. Your son was engaged to Lucy. But she broke it off because she was sick of the way he treated her. Rob's a bully to everybody, including Lucy."

"Oh? Rob's a bully? Well, for your information— and even though I'm strictly against this—even now he's willing to forgive Lucy for running around with that colored boy. Forgive her and take her back. Now does that sound like a bully?"

"He's a regular saint, ain't he?"

He glared at me. "You'll never get the Knolls out of

you, will you, McCain? No matter how successful you become, you'll still be that shabby little Knolls boy."

I leaned against the trunk of my immature ragtop, tapped a Lucky free, and said, "What the hell are you doing here? You didn't come here to tell me to lay off dear sweet Rob. You want something."

He pushed his rimless glasses back up his long nose and said, "I have some information for you."

"Why don't you take it to the police? I'm not interested."

"Clifford's a buffoon. At least you're somewhat intelligent. And Esme and I are bridge partners at the club sometimes."

"I still don't want it."

"Why not?"

I pushed away from the Ford. The summer sunlight fell broken in soft shadows through the trees above. The birds sang with impossible sweetness. And the old garages that lined the other side of the alley behind my building looked like the sort that I'd explored as a kid.

I didn't want to be standing here talking to this prissy prick.

"Anything you say'll be self-serving. You know it's logical that your son is a primary suspect. You also know that it's logical that the police will keep on contacting him until the case is resolved. So you're here to tell me something that's going to put the blame on somebody else. Am I right?"

He looked embarrassed. "You've discredited me even before I had the chance to say anything."

"Then we're done here."

I started to walk toward my office. He caught up with me. He grabbed my shirtsleeve. I pulled my arm away.

"Here's something Rob told me at breakfast this morning. While Neville and Leeds were being killed, my son was visiting his old girlfriend. Her name is Sally Amis and I invite you to call her."

"Were they alone?"

"What difference does that make?"

"It'll make a difference in court. Her word alone won't be good enough, especially if she still has feelings for him. She'd need a witness of her own to corroborate what she says."

"She comes from a good family. She wouldn't lie."

"People lie all the time, good families or not."

"You're missing the point here, McCain. Hannity and Rob weren't together at the time the coroner set for the death. They only got together later. Hannity would have had plenty of opportunity to—"

"I need to get to work, Anderson."

"Your vast law office, huh? I'm sure you'll be sitting on the state supreme court any day now. And be sure to take that stupid secretary you have along with you." Then he chastened himself: "I came here to offer you some help with this case."

"And to get your son off the hook?"

"Well, what if I did, McCain? You'll do the same thing if you ever quit sleeping around and get serious with a decent woman. You'll protect your children just as fiercely as I do."

"Not if they're like your son, I won't."

I went inside.

I NEVER TOLD my dad I didn't care much for hunting mushrooms. I like the outdoors if you have something entertaining to do while you're out there. Mushroom-hunting never fell into that "something entertaining" category for me.

But I always went because it meant I got to be alone with him. And he, or so my mom always said, could maybe forget for a while that my brother had died of polio.

What I liked best about being around him was his stories. His weren't the kind that won you the biggest laughs on Saturday night front porches where the vets from the war gathered. He'd won himself some medals, but he never talked about them. At boot camp he'd saved a buddy's life by dragging him mostly dead from a flooded river. But his stories were rarely about derring-do.

His favorite subject was how radio developed, and I expect just seeing those words set down like that you can see why my father was never a renowned bullshit artist.

But when he'd start talking about how he'd built his first crystal set and how he'd then raised money for his De-pression-era family by building crystal sets for other families, it was fun to hear. And then he'd talk about the Red Network and the Blue Network and how for a long time there was never such a thing as a network that covered the United States all at the same time—the West Coast was usually recorded for later play—and how radio stars like Jack Benny and Edgar Bergen and Charlie McCarthy and the Shadow became just as big as any movie star.

He could also tell you the history of New Orleans

jazz, the evolution of the cowboy movie from the silents to the singing cowboys, the days when Orson Welles was the radio voice of the Shadow, and the ten most memorable days of the big war, Pacific and European; all of it bedazzled me.

I remembered all this as I knelt next to the cot Mom had fixed up for him in the spare room after he got out of the hospital two weeks earlier, the nightstand holding a stack of his beloved Luke Short westerns and two bright yellow packages of Juicy Fruit for when he got the urge to smoke, an urge he would never be able to indulge again.

He slept peacefully, a small and tidy man, his hair gone all to white and that little Irish mug a bit impish even now. The doctor had told me but not Mom (and I wasn't about to tell her, either) that with luck, Dad could live another six, seven months if he didn't have any more major heart attacks. But even without an attack, his heart wasn't going to hold out much longer.

I held his small, coarse, wrinkled hand now and touched my cheek to it. This was when I needed my boyhood faith, my blind certainty there was a God, and for a few moments I banished all cynicism and disbelief. Maybe it wasn't like the believers said, all that angel stuff, but maybe we did live on in some fashion, the essence of each of us anyway, and then I couldn't help it, I touched my cheek to his hand again and started crying.

"HE'S LOOKING GOOD, isn't he?" Mom said, serving my favorite, tomato soup and toasted cheese sandwich.

He had, of course, looked blanched, dead.

"He looks great."

"I know you don't go to Mass anymore, Sam, but I

think you can see what all of us praying has done for your father."

I nodded, spooned some more soup into my mouth. She finally started to eat and I watched her, still the possessor of her young-woman elegance even in a faded housedress; "the prettiest Irish girl of her time" the old monsignor had told me one day as I was cleaning up the altar after serving Mass. I'd wondered if he might have had a crush on her.

But there was no denying the weariness that claimed her. The step a little slower, the response to a question or a remark a few seconds late in coming, and something new of late, sighs so long extended they were like notes in dirges.

"He was talking to Robert again last night just like Robert was alive. He woke me up and I went into the spare room and stood over him and just listened. He was dreaming about that time he built that soapbox derby car for you boys. It was so wonderful hearing him talk like that. He seemed so happy."

She put her hand on mine. "By the way, the judge called here for you late last night. She sounded— confused. I was very polite to her. I told her you hadn't lived here in a long time."

"She was drunk."

"Yes, I'm afraid she was. She's such a fine woman in so many ways. Maybe she needs help."

"She does for sure. It's getting her to accept it that's the problem."

And Mom said what she always says at such moments, "I'll add her to my prayer list, honey."

EIGHTEEN

"Hɪ, ɪs Nᴀɴᴄʏ ʜᴏᴍᴇ?"

Mrs. Adams didn't look happy to see me. She knew who I was and knew that my appearance on the doorstep of her large, Spanish-style home could not mean anything good.

"You're Mr. McCain."

"Yes."

"We know the judge from our club."

"I won't keep her long." I wanted to get on with it. I didn't want to discuss her club or her rather extravagant house or her friendship with the judge.

Mrs. Adams was in her mid-forties, I guessed, so tanned from various trips that her skin was becoming lizardlike in places. She wore large sunglasses with white frames. They were girly and seemed frivolous on a face with a sharp, jutting nose and a mouth made for slander. In her blue walking shorts and sleeveless white blouse, she was every woman you saw playing golf at the country club.

"I think I'm going to refuse."

"That's your prerogative."

"You don't have a very good reputation with people at the club. They've been after the judge to fire you for several years now."

A Negro maid in a crisp gray uniform appeared behind her in the air-conditioned shadows of the large house.

"Good day, Mr. McCain."

"I NEED EVERYTHING you can dig up on Nancy Adams."

"She isn't anybody I've ever heard of before." I could hear Kenny Thibodeau take a deep drag of his cigarette. "I need to finish this chapter. I need to read up on lesbians, I guess. This is lesbian novel number nine and I'm running out of ideas for what they can do in bed."

"That's pretty much what happened to John Steinbeck, wasn't it? Didn't he run out of lesbian ideas for his books?"

"You're just jealous you don't have my career."

"You know, in a weird way I am. I look at all your books in your trailer and I do feel a little pang. That you've been able to start and finish so many of them. The one time I tried to write a novel, I never got past page twenty."

"I didn't know that. How come you never told me?"

"Embarrassed, I guess."

Then Kenny said, "I was going to talk to you later in the day, but I guess I might as well tell you now. You asked me to dig up what I could. So far I've got two real interesting things.

"The first thing is, Richie Neville had two places to work in. His cabin, and then he rented the upper floor of the Parker House, that supper club out on the highway. That was pretty much a secret."

"How'd you find out about it?"

"That was pure Sherlockian fortitude, man. I called

the photo shop where he bought all his supplies. The guy there said that he liked working with Richie and didn't mind delivering to the cabin but that the Parker House took an hour back and forth."

"Good work, Kenny. I have a plaque here with your name on it."

"And then when I was in Iowa City last night, I went over to where David Leeds lived and asked some of his friends about him. They still can't believe he's dead."

"Yeah, so what's the one interesting thing?"

"You know his sister you were talking to?"

"Yeah?"

"They said he didn't have a sister. He was an only child."

"HE WAS THE PERFECT TYPE of renter for us. Real quiet."

"How much time did he spend here?"

"Couple of nights a week, two, three I'd guess."

"He have many visitors?"

"Not that I noticed, anyway. His brother Will."

Ted Wheeler, the owner of the Parker House, had played football for the Iowa Hawkeyes back in the early fifties. He'd known he wasn't good enough for the pros, so he did what so many in sports do, he opened an insurance agency. Who wouldn't want an esteemed Hawkeye as their insurance man?

He'd made so much money with the insurance that he was able to buy an aging restaurant on the highway and turn it into another prosperous business. A bit of a drive for small-town folk not used to driving more than a couple of miles for anything in town, but the drive just seemed to make the evening more special. It was a memorable night going to the Parker House.

I'd found Ted in back of his restaurant hosing off his new, black Jaguar. He was a short, thick man, blond hair thinning now, with a pleasant face that included a badly broken and badly set nose.

The water sparkled rainbows in the late afternoon sunlight and smelled of the rubber hose.

"The police been here to talk to you yet?"

He wiped a massive paw on his T-shirt. "Not yet. I don't think too many people knew about this place."

"I'd appreciate a look."

He shrugged. "Fine by me." He frowned. "He was a nice kid."

I didn't correct him.

"You want me to let you in now?"

"Please."

"I really appreciate how you took care of my sis that time. The dog ripped her leg up pretty good. But then that shit owner brought in that vet who said that she must have done something to rile the dog herself. He looked pretty good on the stand there, but you brought him down right away."

"I didn't have to do much. His story didn't make a lot of sense. And even if she had riled the dog, he was still responsible for what the dog had done."

He twisted the hose off. I followed him up the outside stairs leading to the apartment on the second floor.

The front room must have been half the apartment. New linoleum, throw rugs, a pair of couches covered with matching floral slipcovers, a bookcase packed with a lot of Mickey Spillane and dozens of science fiction titles, a three-foot stack of albums that ran to Elvis and rockabilly types, and a refrigerator-freezer packed with every kind of tasty but spurious TV dinner on the market. With the long front window and light of the fading day, there was a pleasant college-dorm feel to the place.

"I need to get back and get the troops ready for tonight," Ted said. "I always give 'em a little pep talk, you know, like a coach at halftime." He laughed. "They hate it, think it's real corny. But it's a reminder that I expect them to do everything they can to keep the customer happy. You know how that goes. You start out on a job and pretty soon the customer starts looking like the enemy. Hell, I'm the owner and some nights I don't want to wait on certain customers. The real picky ones, I mean. I'm half tempted to say, 'Well, since you find so many things wrong with this place, why don't you go somewhere else?' But I never would, you know what I mean? I've worked too hard to get this place rolling to do anything stupid like that." He gave me a wave. "Good hunting, Sam."

I've always felt self-conscious picking over the bones of the dead. The left-behind letters and photos and books that seem to contradict what you knew of the person. On one job, trying to learn the identity of the man who'd robbed and strangled an eighty-six-year-old longtime widow, I found a fresh pack of Trojans beneath a silk slip; on another investigation, I found a letter written to the deceased man from the child he never knew he'd had until a few weeks before his death. And then there'd been the brutal street cop with a ninth-grade education who'd been killed by a man he'd beaten a false confession out of, the cop belonging to both a classical records club and the Great Books society.

Picking over all these bones through the years, I realized how little we know of each other. We judge each other without having all the information. Many times the quiet life of the soul has little bearing on the noisy life of the body.

But, after an hour of searching, I came to the conclusion that the exterior Richie had been pretty much like the interior one. Girly magazines, several handguns, books on weightlifting and advice on picking up ladies, several photography magazines that did double duty as girly books (the models in the photography magazines infinitely more mysterious and sexual than those in the girly magazines), and six different kinds of aftershave. Apparently the book on picking up ladies swore by aftershave as a tool of seduction.

I found the hidey-hole because I tripped over the register grate in the floor. Its black paint had long ago faded so that the grate was almost gray now. It had collected a furry tissue of dust on it. One thing was out of place. The east end of it was ajar, raised about a quarter inch from the floor. Maybe he'd been in a hurry pushing it down. Or maybe he simply hadn't noticed.

I got down on my knees and went to work. He hadn't made it especially difficult to find the envelopes once you figured that maybe the grate hid, in turn, a more artful hiding place.

My hand went left, my hand went right, waggling, wiggling, crawling until it reached what felt like a large manila envelope that was concealed beneath a piece of cardboard that had been spray-painted black

and then carefully covered with mice turds and large
furry dust devils. You wouldn't look twice at how it had
been concealed. It appeared to be a natural part of the
heating system.

The envelope was heavier than it looked, an 8 x 10
standard issue that had been used for mailing before. It
bore Richie's name and the address of this place.

I grabbed a Falstaff from the refrigerator and seated
myself in an armchair. The contents of the envelope
radiated evil thoughts. I knew I'd found what I was
looking for.

Twenty minutes later, having gone through all
twenty-one photographs, I realized that he hadn't been
much of a Peeping Tom. He hadn't needed to be. Who
needed sweaty naked flesh when it was much easier to
get a couple of simple shots of two adulterous people
holding hands as they left a boathouse or two adulterous people walking into a motel room or two adulterous people furtively kissing goodnight as they stood
between their respective cars. In divorce court, these
would be a bonanza. You didn't need pornography to
make your case. Context alone was enough. Kissing and
holding hands was pretty much a carnal act with photos
like these.

But these weren't local folks. Given the various
settings, I could see that these had been taken in
Chicago. The blackmail franchise had apparently started
in Chicago and had been brought to Black River Falls.

I slid the photos back in the envelope and carried my
beer can to the kitchen counter. The prig side of me had
taken over again. I hated thinking about the misery
these photos had wrought.

NINETEEN

"How did you find out?"

"Guy who writes dirty books found out."

"You have interesting friends."

"And useful."

"Will you be able to believe anything I tell you from now on?"

"It won't be easy."

"My first husband."

"Beg pardon?"

"He had an affair right after we got married. Right after. I found out and tried to leave him. He convinced me to stay for three months and give it a try. But it didn't work."

"Because you couldn't believe him. You were suspicious all the time."

"You've been through it?"

"Both ends of the gun. Cheater and cheatee. Once somebody lies to you it's hard to believe them again."

"Maybe next time around I should try being the one who cheats."

Marie Leeds's hotel had a taproom full of road-weary salesmen, half of whom stood at one end of the bar and told dirty jokes, the other half of whom sat at the bar and stared at their drinks, as if by trying hard enough maybe they could levitate them.

We were sitting at one of those knee-knocking little cocktail tables that get wobbly pretty fast. A candle encased in a tube of red glass flicked rose-colored light across our faces.

"How about we start with your real name, since you aren't really his sister."

"The first name really is Marie."

"Gosh, I know we're on the right track now."

"And my last name is Denham."

"And you knew David Leeds how?"

She leaned back and picked up her package of Tareytons, got one going, put an explosion of smoke in my direction, and said, "I was his English teacher in high school. He came from a bad home situation. I sort of adopted him. I gave him the small apartment above my garage and that's where he spent his senior year."

"His folks didn't have any objections?"

"His father was dead. His mother was an alcoholic and not easy to get along with. We had our battles, she and I. David made the mistake of telling her he had a crush on me. It didn't last long, but the damage was done."

"She thought you were sleeping together?"

"Yes."

"Were you?"

She smiled. It was slow and sweet, that smile, suggestive of whatever you wanted it to suggest. "I wish I could say yes. Maybe things would've turned out differently. David was extremely impulsive. He never got into big trouble, but he certainly got into his share of scrapes. Maybe it would have allowed me to keep tighter control of him." The smile slowly disappeared. "But, no, I didn't. My mama didn't raise me to do things like that."

"Why did you register at the hotel here as Leeds?"

"Because I was pretending to be his sister."

"You mentioned scrapes. What kind of scrapes?"

"Girl scrapes mostly." She smiled. "He wasn't just handsome. He was Negro and handsome. A lot of white girls were curious about that. But he also got into scrapes out here. Somebody at the hotel told me David caught Hannity cutting the tires of his scooter. I guess Hannity's a pretty big guy. But David was so mad he plowed right into him."

"When was this?"

"My understanding is that it was a couple of weeks ago."

Rob Anderson's father had hinted that Hannity might be worth checking into. The two young men hadn't been together during the time of the murders. This had all been self-serving, a dad trying to help his son, but Marie had given me one more reason to look Hannity up again.

"I'll be lucky if I don't get my own tires slashed. I rented a car this afternoon and drove around. Most of the people were very nice to me. But there're a few— they always want you to apologize somehow for existing because you're different than they are. And they think they know you just because of your skin color. And worst of all, they hate you. You can see it in their eyes. You're something vile to them. I'm not sure I could live in your town."

"You just said it was a minority of people who were like that."

"That's all it takes, Sam. A handful. Being just as hateful as they can be. The Klan doesn't have all that many members, but they've never been stronger because we're finally standing up for our rights. It doesn't take many bad guys to cause a lot of pain and consternation. Look at poor Medgar Evers."

"I'm sorry for the bad ones you met here." I laughed but without pleasure. "The old love-hate thing I have for this town. Most of the folks here are decent. Not saints, nothing like that. Decent people. But there are always a few—"

"Hannity and Anderson might get away with it because their people have money and influence."

"In most cases, money and influence can buy you out of trouble. But not a double murder like this. Every paper in the state is covering this. The race angle's in everybody's mind. Anybody who's charged will be prosecuted right up to the maximum sentence."

She put her cigarettes in her purse and sat up straight, with her hands folded in front of her. She was ready to shove off.

"Those Freedom Riders, that's why most people around here'll want to see justice. Even some of the folks who hate us see what's happening to the riders and Dr. King and they know it's not right. They're doing our suffering for us."

"You're probably right. A lot of the haters probably don't like watching fire hoses and dogs put on little kids."

Her smile was bitter. "Thank God for the wee ones. They can get to adults the way we can't. It's the old plantation thing—the pickaninnies sure are cute till they grow up. Then they're just more colored folks to put the lash to. David paid the price for that. He stayed real cute right into his twenties and somebody around here didn't like that. Didn't like that at all."

TWENTY

CLAMMY SWEAT. Otherworld darkness. Nightmare. My conscious mind trying to reject—to banish—the hellish sounds that forced blood to run dripping from my ears. The cats were in my nightmare, too, each of them crawling beneath the covers to free themselves from the tortured voice that refused to stop.

And then I was sitting up and wide awake the way movie people always are right after nightmare time. Disoriented for a few moments. Trying to comfort the cats that now clung to me as if I were their father.

And still that noise—

Aw, shit.

And then I realized what it was. Kenny Thibodeau's new girlfriend Noreen De Grasso, who fancied herself the nation's only serious rival to Joan Baez in the folksong singing business.

Trying to untwist my boxers, I stomped over to the open window next to the back door. Had to be 100 degrees in here and it was nearly ten at night. The window air conditioner Mrs. Goldman had bought for my apartment was brand-new not long ago and was already in the shop getting repaired. She'd let me pick out the one I wanted. Some picker-outer.

I found a pack of smokes on the kitchen counter and

fired one up before I yelled down there and told them to cool it.

But the way they were passing that half-gallon jug of Gallo back and forth, it was unlikely they even heard me.

Finally Kenny looked up and saw me in the window and waved.

"Hey, man, we'll be right up!"

This was how I'd lived for six, seven months—this being a few years before even Mary dumped me—after it became clear that the beautiful Pamela Forrest and I were never getting married. I had planned, in my early twenties, to try to become something remotely resembling a grown-up. But the heartbreak was such that all I wanted was to stay numb. Kenny was eager to show me the wastrel route and I went along willingly.

That six or seven months was a frenzy of self-indulgence that was at least manic and maybe even clinical. In memory, everything runs speeded up, the way the old silent films look to us today.

Piling in and out of cars, apartments, movie theaters, taverns, the abodes of girls you were somewhat serious about, the girls you selfishly used for lonely sex (and who were using you right back the same way)—anything and everything was never enough. Two hours' sleep before you went to work? No sweat, man. Your car never having more than a quarter tank of gas because you'd spent all your money on girls and beer? Cool. Waking up on the floors of strangers and strangers waking up on your couch and pissed in their psycho hangovers because you weren't serving breakfast, and their girlfriends commandeering your toilet for an hour or two—

And the people you only vaguely remember through the haze of alcohol—my haze was pretty transparent; two beers and I was drunk and doing my yodeling impression—loners and losers and grotesques and dangerous people who somehow stayed with your group through barhopping, dancing, pissing in tavern parking lots, breaking up fights, starting fights—somehow they were always with you. One night this guy pulled a knife on Kenny because he said Kenny's porno was grabbing the money and attention that he, the knife-wielder, should rightly claim for his own writing, which just happened to be Literature. Another night I'm in bed with this girl who was far gone drunk but still very sexy and when I rolled over there was a steely lump of something beneath the sheets and it turned out to be a .38 because "I always take a gun along with me the first time I sleep with a guy because he might be, you know, creepy or something." True tales of the bedroom. Would-be communists, anarchists, pregnant girls stepping out on their husbands (more true bedroom tales), and of course the entire range of ex-cons you always stumble on in the taverns where the girls go.

But all this was in another part of the galaxy. Whoever that moron had been who'd lived that way sure wasn't me anymore. I just gave it all up and went back to being a pretty serious young man.

Kenny hadn't.

So they tromped up the stairs and I grabbed a pair of Levi's cutoffs and slammed a six-pack of Schlitz down on the coffee table and readied myself for the siege.

Coming through the door, Noreen said, "Man, do I have to take a dump!"

Kenny howled. "Isn't she something?"

"'Something.' I think you hit it, Kenny. You know what time it is?"

"Aw, hell. Relax."

He helped himself to one of the beers on the coffee table and said, leaning forward, "You know what she did, man?"

I was afraid to ask.

"She wrote a song for you." He put a finger to his lips and went sssh. "But act surprised when she tells you."

Could this be real? Maybe this was one of those real tricky nightmares that went on for a long time.

I hate the prig side of me. The unkind, snotty thoughts. But Noreen brought them out in me. It wasn't just her singing. She always wore short skirts and no underwear and when she sprawled on my couch it was impossible not to look. She just helped herself to whatever she wanted from fridge or cupboard. And a couple of nights she asked if she could sleep on my couch because she was pissed at Kenny. And she didn't bathe very often. She said she had read an article in some health magazine—one can only imagine what kind of magazine that was—that if you bathed or showered more than once a week you caused a "frisson on your epidermis." And as she always said when she was finishing up, "A lot of scientists are signing on to that, McCain. This isn't just, you know, bullshit or anything." I was pretty sure that most of these "scientists" had probably been educated on the lost continent of Atlantis.

And one more thing—as I heard her exploding from

the bathroom door—she never washed her hands after attending to her toilet needs.

"You asshole," she said, "I heard you telling him I wrote a song about him." She whacked him pretty hard across the back of the head. He giggled.

She jumped on the couch, managing to snag her acoustic guitar in the process, and landed with enough force to make one end of the couch jump a quarter inch. What's remarkable about this is that she weighed only about a hundred pounds. She was five-two, junkie-thin, with scraggly black hair down to her ass and a face that was pretty in a sort of psycho way. Not even Norman Bates could have claimed eyes as crazy as her baby-blues.

Whenever I saw Noreen and Kenny together, I wondered how Kenny could have given up his former longtime girlfriend Cindy Baines, a sweet, smart, pretty nurse who loved Kenny in a way that was moving to see. But Cindy hadn't wanted the abortion he browbeat her into having. And after that things weren't right. She spent several long evenings at my house telling me how much she loved him but also how much she felt sad about the abortion. She still wanted to marry Kenny, but she wanted him to understand how the abortion had devastated her. Ultimately everything came to a sad end and Cindy moved to Omaha.

As for Kenny …

As she strummed her guitar in preparation for the song she'd written for me, she said, "Did Kenny tell you I'm in regression therapy now?"

"No, he didn't mention that. I guess I'm not sure what that is."

"You know, like they take you back to past lives."

"This shit is so cool," Kenny said. "I'm gonna try it for myself."

"I was an Egyptian princess."

"Isn't that cool?" Kenny said, chugging beer. "She's an Egyptian princess."

This was bringing back all those insane nights in my degenerate period. Everybody was so drunk or so stoned on bad marijuana that everything that was said made a kind of sense. *Did he just say he kept a dolphin under his bed? Did she just say that she was a telepath? Did he just say that he'd once fought Rocky Marciano and beat the crap out of him?* Sure, why not, everybody was so stupid on booze and grass, anything that was said was perfectly fine. Down the rabbit hole.

So why not an Egyptian princess?

Every time I was around Noreen I realized, despite feeling like an outsider, how middle-class I really was.

"So go on, Noreen. Play him the song you wrote about him."

I prepared my face to contort itself into an expression of seeming pleasure that would extend from the first to the last note she played. What choice did I have? I had to like it, didn't I?

"You know the song 'John Henry,' Sam?" Noreen said.

"'John Henry was a steel-drivin' man'? Sure."

"Well, that's what this is pretty much except it's 'Sam McCain was a law-abidin' man till they pushed him too far.'"

That was another thing about Noreen's songs. They were never Noreen's songs. She purloined the music from famous songs and just rewrote the lyrics, most of which were so radical politically they made me feel positively GOP.

"The deal is, see, in this song," Kenny, ever helpful, said, "you bring this innocent man to court but the corrupt jury that's bought off by the robber barons, they find this guy guilty. And so you track every one of the jurors down and shoot 'em."

"Great," I said. "A mass murderer."

"See, you screwed it up again, Kenny," Noreen said. "The last one he doesn't shoot, he stabs."

"Oh, sorry, babe." To me: "The last one you stab."

"Got it. The last one I stab."

I don't know about you folks but I believe in miracles. Big miracles and sort of smaller, everyday miracles alike. I mention this because right then the phone rang.

"Don't answer that," Kenny said.

"Why the hell not?"

"Because she's psyched to sing you your song."

The phone continuing to ring.

"He's right, Sam. I'm ready now." Starting to strum again. Ready. Psyched.

I picked up the phone.

"Am I calling too late?" Jane Sykes said.

"No. Not at all."

Kenny was pantomiming "hang up" with his hand slamming down an invisible phone. Noreen was rolling her eyes at me and looking generally disgusted with humankind, especially those who served on juries.

"Have you heard what happened tonight?"

And I saw how I could get rid of them.

"Hold on a minute. I didn't realize this was going to be official business," I said to Jane and set the phone down. I stood up and said, "I'm sorry but you'll have to leave. This is something I have to deal with alone."

"Can't you take the phone into the crapper?" Noreen said. "We couldn't hear it then."

"Much as I enjoy sitting in the crapper, the phone cord doesn't reach that far, Noreen."

I grabbed the phone and said to Jane, "Just one more minute." I put the receiver down and said, "C'mon now, you guys, you gotta leave."

"Well, this is really bullshit," Noreen said.

"She was really psyched."

"I write a whole goddamn song for him and he kicks me out," Noreen said to herself.

But Kenny, finally understanding how pissed I was, grabbed her hand and started dragging her toward the back door.

"I write a song just for him and—"

I missed the rest because the door had slammed on her. Kenny was still on the inside of the door: "This is pretty rude, man."

"Is it as rude as waking somebody up on a work night to play some lousy song?"

"Lousy? You haven't even heard it yet."

Kenny and I have had a love-hate relationship since grade school. We were definitely in hate mode now.

"'Night, Kenny," I said, pushing the door open and giving him a little shove into the night.

The last thing I heard from them was Noreen strumming and singing "Sam McCain was a law-abidin' man till they pushed him too far." I was glad I couldn't hear anything more.

Back on the phone, Jane said, "I'm sorry if I interrupted anything."

"Just a murder."

"What?"

"A double murder, actually. Two people who woke me up and decided to have a party. So what's going on?"

"Rachael Todd—the one we thought was killed because she was going to tell you something about Leeds and Neville?"

"Yeah."

"A sixty-six-year-old woman walked into Cliff's office tonight—of course Cliff wasn't there—and confessed to being the hit-and-run driver. She was coming back from her sister's and realized that she couldn't see very well without her glasses but assumed she could make it home without any problem. Well, there was a problem. Rachael Todd sort of stumbled out in front of the woman's car and that's how the woman hit her. The woman's name by the way is Dot Taylor, and the deputy who looked over her car said you can still see blood and a little bit of hair on the right front bumper and fender."

"I don't know if this is good news or bad news. You know, in mystery novels you're never supposed to have a coincidence like this."

"Well, I guess it gives us one less thing to worry about."

"But we still don't know what she was going to tell me."

A pause. "I notice you said 'me.'"

"Oh. Right."

"I was under the assumption that we were still working together. I haven't heard from you in a while."

"Well, I've been—"

"Before you tell a lie, which will really piss me off, let me tell you what's going on. She got to you, didn't she?"

"She?"

"God, c'mon, Sam. Just admit it. The judge found out that we were together socially and got all uptight about it. Right?"

My turn to pause. "Yeah, right."

"And so she just naturally extrapolated from there that we were probably working together, too."

"Pretty much."

"And you gave in to her."

I took a long time to answer it. "The judge and I have a very complicated relationship. She helped me when I set up shop and nobody else would. She helped me get my private investigator's license, which isn't easy in this state. And she's steered a lot of business my way."

"You gave in to her."

"And she's—she's in a kind of strange position now. She needs some help."

"Her drinking."

"Are you mocking me here?"

Extended sigh. "A little, I guess. I mean you're making it sound more like a love affair than a business relationship. But I apologize, Sam. I guess it hurts my pride that you chose her over me. But that makes sense. You've been friends—or whatever you are—for a long time."

"That doesn't mean we can't see each other socially."

Nervous laugh. "I probably screwed that up for us, Sam."

"How?"

"I said a lot of awkward things the first night we met. I was trying not to flirt with you but it sort of came out that way, and I'm sorry it did. The truth is, Sam, I don't know what I'm looking for—if I'm looking for anything. I like to work hard because then I don't have to think about it. I like you very much, but you're very different from the other men I've been with. There weren't that many—three, really—but they ran to a type and you don't fit that type at all. And you're so different from them and—"

"What type are we talking about?"

"Oh, it's not worth discussing. See, right there I said something I shouldn't have."

"Tall, dark, and handsome? Is that the type we're talking about?"

Pause. "Believe it or not, yes. It just seemed to work out that way. And it was very flattering, I have to say."

"But you're beautiful."

"Well, I'm attractive. I don't know about beautiful."

"So it's logical handsome men would be attracted to you." Pause. "Let me ask you something personal about them."

"Well, if it's not too personal."

"Were any of them ever nicknamed 'Yosemite Sam'?"

I thought she might not have understood the reference, but after a hesitation she broke into a full-throated laugh. "That's just what I mean, Sam. You saved the moment because you're so witty."

"And short."

"Well—"

"And not handsome—"

"In your way you are."

"And not dark. Fish-belly white and freckled in places."

"You really know how to sell yourself."

But then it was done. I could sense it. I'd kidded it along so we could both save face, and much as we enjoyed that moment, we both realized that it was one of those fireflies that only glow for a minute or so.

"I just don't want to hurt you, if we go out socially I mean."

"I understand."

"I think I'm pretty good company sometimes, but I don't know if it can ever be more than that for us."

"Well, let's think on it."

"I'm sorry if I hurt your feelings."

"You didn't. You were honest is all."

"Well, I probably should go. We both need our sleep. I just wanted to make sure you'd heard about Rachael Todd."

"I appreciate the call, Jane."

"We'll talk soon, Sam."

"'Night."

For a long time I just sat in the chair. The cats came and sat on me. I was looking for a bride these days— now that I was trying to be an adult again, and at age twenty-six it was past time—but maybe in looking so earnestly I'd lost whatever charm I'd once held for women. Trying too hard, to make it simple.

I spent a few minutes working out with self-pity,

spreading it throughout my body, saturating every cell of my being and mind with it, and then I stood up and turned off the lights and went to the back door to make sure it was locked.

And it was then I heard it. And for the first time there was a sweetness to Noreen's voice. Maybe it was because this particular song was about a lost love and not shooting cops or burning nuns or building monuments to Stalin.

This was a young woman singing about a love affair she couldn't rid herself of. And it had an old hill-country quality—a good many townspeople were from folks who'd migrated here from the Ozarks following the Civil War, the kin of whom still lived in the section where I'd grown up—that particular sadness of the poor and the uneducated and the trapped that the Irish and the Scotch had carried with them on their boats to the new country.

I'd never heard any of these qualities in her voice or manner before and so I grabbed the last six-pack and went down to the old rocker porch swing that Mrs. Goldman had put near the alley and joined them.

And limned by starlight and soothed by wind and startled by the beauty of her voice when she sang this type of song, I became in those moments a fan of Noreen's, something that verged on the impossible.

"I'D LIKE TO see her."

"She specifically asked that you not see her."

"I don't believe that."

"That was what Dr. Berryman told us. In fact, there he is now. You can ask him yourself."

Hospital. Six-thirty a.m. Sights and sounds and smells of the new day. Crisp nurses, preoccupied doctors studying notes and charts. Gurneys being pushed toward one of three operating rooms at the far end of this hall. A glimpse into the room where loved ones waited for word of how the surgery went. Tense faces. Tears. A young man hugging a frail elderly woman.

The nurse I'd been speaking to pointed to Berryman, who had just stepped off an elevator and was just starting down the hall in the opposite direction.

I caught up with him. We'd known each other professionally for three or four years. He was a small man in his forties with a somber face and a cordial manner.

"She's going to be all right, Sam. But it's going to be a while before she's back on the bench."

"I don't even know what happened. I just got a call from her driver that she'd been in an accident and was in the hospital."

He frowned. Leaned in, quieted his voice. "She's got to face it this time, Sam. She was coming home from the club alone and ran off the road out by Simpson's Peak."

"That ravine?"

He nodded. "She'd be dead if she hadn't run into the pine tree that's right down from the top. Nobody found her till about four this morning. She'd lost a lot of blood. She's also got a broken hip, a broken arm, and a concussion."

"Is she awake?"

He studied me a moment. "Sam, the way she tells it,

the reason she got so drunk at the club last night was because she'd had some kind of falling-out with you. She said she didn't trust you any longer." Then: "She wanted me to be sure and tell you that." One of his infrequent smiles. "Working the old guilt routine on you. Esme's drunk every night of the week no matter what happens in her life, good or bad."

"She wanted you to tell me that but she doesn't want to see me." Alcoholics always blame other people.

"That's what she says anyway, and in her condition, I didn't want to argue with her. For one thing, we gave her a lot of pain medication, so she's not thinking clearly. And for another, you're just a handy excuse, as I said."

A nurse passed by and smiled at me. Former client of mine. Happily remarried after I helped her win an unchallenged divorce. Another wife abuse case.

"Sam, you're closer to her than anybody."

"Than her friends at the country club?"

"I'm one of those friends at the country club. We all care for Esme a great deal, but we really don't know her, even after all these years. You know how she holds herself back. Even when she's drunk and staggering around, she never divulges anything personal. And she's at the end, Sam. She can't go on drinking. Her body won't let her. Her liver—" He made a face. "You work with her. You have influence with her. You're the only one we can think of who can get her into that clinic. If she doesn't go through that program and give up the bottle, our Esme won't live another year. Two at the very outside. And believe me, they won't be pretty years either. Not for her or anybody around her."

His name was announced in that sterile tone of all hospital announcements.

"Give her a day or two, Sam. Then come back and see her. I need to go."

Judge Whitney submitting herself to the structure and vagaries of a clinic. Life lived at the mercy of somebody else's rules. Unthinkable.

PART THREE

TWENTY-ONE

"Good morning, Mr. C."

"'Morning, Jamie."

"My birthday is next week. And guess where Turk is taking me?"

"The Dairy Queen?"

She laughed. "No, a birthday is a big event. He's taking me to see Frankie Avalon."

"Is Frankie Avalon still around?"

"He is in Des Moines. Don't you like him?"

"He's all right. But I'd take Chuck Berry, personally."

"He puts too much grease on his hair. Like Jerry Lewis."

I knew this could go on forever, so I said, "Any calls?"

"Just one. Nancy Adams."

I got myself seated behind my desk, scanned down the "To Do" list I always make for myself the day before.

"You want her phone number?"

"Sure." She gave it to me and I dialed. "Nancy Adams, please. This is Sam McCain returning her call."

"Dammit," the woman said, after cupping the phone. Or kind of cupping the phone. "Your father and I told you not to call him." I couldn't hear what Nancy said.

The woman again: "May she call you back? She's washing her hair right now."

"Or I could call her back."

"Well, actually we have to run a few errands after she's finished with her hair. And she'll call you after that. Good-bye, Mr. McCain."

"Did you take the call from Nancy Adams or did the service?" I asked after hanging up.

"The service. It came in before I got here."

I dialed the three digits to connect with our answering service. "Hi, this is Sam. Did you take the call from a Nancy Adams?"

"Yes, I did, Mr. McCain."

"Did she say anything other than she'd like me to call her back?"

"Not really. Except—"

"Except what?"

"Well, I sort of had the impression she was sort of nervous. It was her tone, I mean. She didn't say anything specific. She just sounded real uptight."

"Thanks, Betty."

I had three briefs I had to read before I could spend any time on the Leeds murder. Or on what I was going to say to Judge Whitney when the time came to go up and see her and bring up the subject of the clinic in Minnesota.

In the next two hours I caught up on everything pressing. I'd told Jamie to tell everybody I was out. She knew the exceptions were Judge Whitney and my folks. Right now, she didn't have to worry about the judge.

When I finished, I leaned back in my chair and started mentally plotting out my argument for court tomorrow morning. An especially ugly divorce case. I represented a mill worker who, in response to the affair his wife was having, took their three-year-old daughter for the weekend without telling anybody (a) that he did it, or (b) that he was taking a hotel room in Cedar Rapids.

It was easy to portray the wife as a woman of soiled virtue. But I knew John, the husband, was almost psychotically suspicious of her and had made their lives hell from the start of their marriage. John was a decent man and Sandy was a decent woman. She claimed she was justified in having an affair because he'd had so many himself. The joys of divorce court. Plenty of psychic pain and blame to go around with the kids in the middle.

She came in just before lunchtime.

Turk had made his usual appearance ("Hey, Mr. C, you always look so busy, man, you should relax more.") his black leather jacket looking like something from *West Side Story* rather than *The Blackboard Jungle*.

A few minutes after Turk and Jamie left, Nancy Adams stood in the doorway and said, "Are you busy, Mr. McCain?"

"Hi, Nancy."

She smiled nervously, a perfect young woman, slim in tan walking shorts and a starched white blouse, possessed of long, tanned arms and legs and a small earnest face. Her dark hair was worn short in a shag. "I wondered if we could talk a little bit."

"Sure."

"Don't think badly of my mom. She just doesn't want to see me dragged into court or anything. That's why she said what she did on the phone." A voice as soft as her brown eyes.

"I know my office isn't much, but don't be afraid to come inside." She was still standing on the threshold.

"Oh, right."

She came in and took one of the client chairs. "I don't know if I'm doing the right thing."

"If you're telling the truth, then that's the right thing."

"That sounds like something you'd hear on TV."

I laughed. "A little pompous?"

She smiled. She was blushing. "I probably shouldn't have said that." I'd been doing that lately—beginning to sound like Dear Abby.

"I have some pop in the refrigerator."

"No, thanks." Still busy with her hands. "I guess I may as well just tell you, huh?"

"Probably best, yes."

She sat up a little straighter. "Well, you know I go out with Nick Hannity. Or I should say, used to go out with him."

"You broke up?"

"Yes. He—he told you and the police that he was with me during the time David Leeds and Richie Neville were being killed out at the cabin."

"Yes, he did."

"Well, he wasn't. I didn't see him till much later that night." She took a deep breath. "And the fact is, he hated David. One night when David and Lucy were having some problems, David came over to my house and we just talked. My folks—please don't think they're bad people because they're not—they were pretty mad about him coming over like that. You know, with my dad's position and all, he said if people thought I was going out with a Negro then they wouldn't want to do business with him anymore."

Another deep breath. "In fact—and this was really embarrassing—David and I were sitting out on the front porch talking and my dad came out and said he wanted to talk to me. He was very cold to David. Wouldn't say hello or anything after David was so polite to him and everything. Anyway, my dad got me inside the front door and he was so mad he didn't care if David heard him or not. He just ranted and raved at me the way he does sometimes. He said some very mean things about colored people and David in particular. David couldn't help but hear him. He told me to go back out there and get rid of David in five minutes or he'd come out there and get rid of him himself. I was afraid to go back out after all the terrible things he said but I didn't have any choice."

"What did David say when you went back to the porch?"

"He didn't say anything. He was gone." She shook her head. "That was the last time I ever saw him. But that wasn't all."

"When was this, by the way?"

"Two nights before they were killed."

"Fine. Now you said there was something else, too?"

She sat up straight again. "I'd been taking some time off from Nick. He was a year older and he was one of the really cool guys in high school and everybody always told me how lucky I was to be going with him— I just always thought we'd get married. But then I started going to the university in Iowa City and seeing him constantly and—I didn't like him. I always knew he was sort of a bully, but it really came out when he was on campus. And he got mad if I even said hello to some guy. So when Rob told him about Lucy seeing David—he went insane. He had no reason to be jealous of anything. Even if I'd had a crush on David, I'm not sure how I feel about dating Negroes—I'm being honest here—and I'd sure never date any boy, white or colored, who looked like David."

"Why not?"

"Just too good-looking. Girls were always making passes at him and right in front of Lucy. I just couldn't have dealt with that."

"How did Nick find out that David had been at your house?"

"My dad told him when Nick came over on his motorcycle that night. You should've heard Nick. I was really scared. He wanted to go and find David right then. He kept saying he was going to kill him." She started picking at her fingers.

The phone rang. I excused myself and picked it up. Kenny Thibodeau. "A little news for you. The afternoon Neville and Leeds were shot to death, Rob Anderson asked Ned Flannery to make him up a good-sized 'tar baby' with a rope around its neck." Flannery was a local artisan. "Ned wouldn't do it, of course. Anderson offered him a hundred bucks."

I saw Nancy glancing at her watch. She started to stand up. "Hang on a minute, Kenny."

"I'd better go. I'm s'posed to meet my mom in a few minutes. I'm pretty much done, anyway."

"Well, thanks for coming in. I really appreciate it."

As she left, Kenny said, "Pretty sick, huh?"

"Very."

"I wonder if he got somebody to do it for him."

"I'll ask him when I see him."

"Man, I get all hepped up watchin' TV and all the Freedom Riders and thinkin' everybody will get behind all this, they'll see what bullshit racism is. But it's like bein' stoned when you think like that—because when you come down again, nothin's changed. People're gettin' tar babies made."

"It's hard to watch TV anymore. You want to put your fist through the screen."

I heard Kenny strike a match and light a cigarette. "That was pretty cool last night. Those old mountain songs, huh? You still gotta hear this Bob Dylan guy. He's as good as Woody Guthrie."

I laughed. "You'll guarantee that?"

I WENT OVER and locked the door. Jamie wouldn't be back for another fifteen minutes.

The wall safe was behind a framed reproduction of an Edward Hopper painting. I pulled the frame back on its hinges and went to work on the safe. It was good-sized. When I got it open, I pulled out the manila envelopes with the blackmail negatives. Four envelopes.

I set them on my desk, grabbed the phone book, and went to work. I had sealed them all with extra-heavy tape. I hadn't looked inside. It wasn't that I was such a moral person. I just didn't want to know what the negatives would tell me. Because once I knew, it would change my attitude, however subtly, toward the people in the pictures. And two of them, excluding the senator, I considered myself at least casual friends with.

I called each name on the envelopes and said that I'd
come into possession of something that Richie Neville
had inadvertently left in my office. I wondered if they'd
like to stop by and pick it up between five and seven
tonight. I gave them each specific times to be here.
They all agreed to appear.

Most important, I said that I hadn't had time to look
at the contents and that there'd be no charge. They all
sounded relieved. One woman started crying and saying
thank you so often, she sounded like the lucky contest-
ant on a quiz show.

The flower shop was nearby. I decided to see if Lucy
was working.

KAREN PORTER SAID, "I still think you should have a nice
fresh flower for your lapel. I hear judges are impressed
by things like that."

She was always fun to clown with. "Not any judges
I know on this planet."

The small shop was filled as always with the sights
and scents of dozens of flowers, arrangements, and
potted plants. A pair of women in straw hats were
dawdling over carnations while the little boy with them
looked as if he'd suddenly found himself in hell.

Karen, in her usual crisp white button-down shirt,
long blue apron, and chignon, still looked as if she
should be in a fancy wine ad in *The New Yorker.* New
England, modest wealth, intelligence, quiet beauty.

"You lucked out, Sam. Ellen's off running errands."

"Am I going to get you in trouble if I go in the back
and talk to Lucy?"

"Not if you happened to have snuck in the back door

and I didn't happen to see it." She frowned. "I don't know why Ellen has to see you as the enemy."

To me the reason was obvious. Ellen was afraid that Lucy might have killed David Leeds and Richie Neville. Lucy had said herself that David had wanted to break it off. I represented a threat to Ellen and her daughter.

"I appreciate it, Karen."

"Just don't get me involved. That lady has got a temper."

"I DON'T THINK you're supposed to be here, Mr. McCain."

Lucy, in jeans and a black Hawkeye T-shirt, was using a spritzer to water rows of plants.

"I just wanted to see how you were doing."

"How do you *think* I'm doing? That's sort of a stupid question, isn't it?"

"Now that you mention it, it is. I apologize."

"It's like those stupid reporters asking parents how they feel when something's happened to one of their kids. 'How do you feel?' That really pisses me off, being that insensitive."

The rear of the shop had been built as an afterthought, a shedlike area that housed two huge refrigerated glassed-in cases to keep flowers fresh and then plants and seedlings sitting on sawhorses that had been covered with plywood.

"Have you talked to Rob?"

"Not if I can help it."

Spritz, spritz.

Lucy said: "I did talk to David's sister. She called me and we had coffee. I liked her very much."

I didn't tell her of David's real relationship with his "sister."

"So do I. I just wish I had some news for her."

"A lot of the kids around town think it was Rob."

"Or Nick."

Spritz, spritz.

"Or Nick."

The smell of damp earth brought back a memory of my Uncle Bob's funeral. He'd died in Korea. When they buried him here, a light rain had given the grave dirt a particular odor. I smelled that odor here, now, with the spritzed dirt in the various plants.

"You know anything about Rob trying to get a tar baby made up?"

She nodded, still not looking at me. "Oh, yes. I heard all about it from a couple of people at the craft store. Good old Rob. God, I don't know how I could've gone out with him all that time."

I said, as carefully as possible, "I guess I never really asked you."

"Well, then, I'm sure you will. Whatever it is."

"I just need to know, just to keep everybody equal, where you were the night Neville and David were killed."

Now she looked up. "Why, I was out at Neville's cabin, killing them. I'm surprised it took you this long to ask. So do you put handcuffs on me here or do we wait until we get in your car?"

"You could've done it, Lucy. You know that."

"You stupid ass," she said, pushing me aside so she could reach another tray of seedlings. "I loved him. I was willing to destroy my father's career because of him. Why would I kill him?"

Karen appeared in the doorway. She was irritated: "Hold it down, you two. We've got customers, for God's sake."

"Sorry," I said.

I left Lucy alone for a few minutes.

"You told me yourself that he wanted to break it off." I spoke in a stage whisper.

As did she. "Break it off because he thought that marrying him—and yes, that's exactly what I had in mind—would destroy me. He didn't think I was strong enough to handle it in the long run."

I touched her sleeve. She jerked away. "I had to ask. I just want to know what happened."

"What happened"—and here she pushed her beautiful face close to my unbeautiful one—"is this society is so racist it won't even let you marry the person you love. That's what happened." She pulled back. Visibly forced herself to calm down. "If we'd just been two white people, we could have had a wonderful life together. But David was right. That would never happen. Not in this country, anyway. No matter where we went, somebody would get ugly either with us or the kids we had. That's what happened. Somebody just couldn't stand the idea that David and I were together. And so they killed him."

Her voice had steadily risen.

Karen was in the doorway again: "Dammit, you two!"

I waved at her. And left.

I WAS WALKING BACK to my office when somebody behind me called my name. I wasn't familiar enough with her voice to recognize it yet. Jane Sykes.

"Mind some company?"

"Be my guest."

"You sound kind of mad."

"Confused more than mad."

"I really did lay it on pretty heavy."

"Yeah, you did."

"I'm just protecting you and protecting me."

"More you than me."

"Stated just like a lawyer."

We were across the street from the town square. Kids splashing in the wading pool, retirees playing checkers and throwing horseshoes, teenage boys aching for the teenage girls they saw passing by. As much as I wanted to be an adult, I had flashbacks to when the mode of transportation was a Schwinn and you could find a girl who'd ride on your handlebars as you pretended to be in complete control of the bike that was about to go careening into a tree. Memory is a lie, but not a complete lie.

Two decades of cars crawled down the crowded street. I loved the prewar coupes, the preferred cars for pulp cover gangsters riding on the running boards with their guns blazing; the big unapologetic Packards that announced to one and all that even if you didn't own the entire world, you owned a damn good share of it; and the 1955 Chevrolets, the most radical departure from the accepted look in automobile history. The languid dusty sunlight on them all gave them a feel of being trapped inside a museum.

"So why don't you buy me dinner tonight, see how it goes?"

"I dunno, Jane."

"Oh, God."

"What?"

"I run hot and cold and now you run hot and cold?"

"How about I call you later?"

"All right. But I'll be at Cliff's most of the afternoon. I've asked him to bring Rob Anderson in. Or haven't you heard about the tar baby?"

"Yeah, apparently the whole town has."

She broke into long strides that pulled her far away from me in less than a minute. In less than forty-eight hours I'd gone through love at first sight, fear, embarrassment, wanton sexual need, and rage with her. Sounded like the basis for a promising relationship.

TWENTY-TWO

By 6:45 ALL BUT ONE of my blackmail subjects had shown up and taken a manila envelope. Two of them tried to disguise themselves in slouch hats and heavy coats. In this kind of weather they looked suspicious as hell.

But it was a happy time for them and they thanked me.

The senator hadn't shown up yet. Given how eager he'd been the morning he'd worn his own disguise, I was surprised he chose to be late.

I kept watching the office door. I also kept watching the office phone. I thought maybe Jane Sykes would decide to call me, since I'd decided not to call her.

I didn't waste time, though. I had plenty of paperwork to shuffle through and I kept busy right up until 7:20. The senator was now thirty-five minutes late.

I went down the hall to the john, washed up, and combed my hair. Somehow a Swanson TV dinner didn't sound so good. I decided I'd go to the steak house out on the highway.

I'd left my office door open. I'd also left the lights on. Now the lights were off. This would have alarmed me more if the electrical wiring in this building hadn't been done by Ben Franklin himself.

The first thing was to get to the fuses Jamie kept in her desk. I was two steps across the threshold when someone moved from the shadows and smashed something hard across the side of my head.

It wasn't a clean knockout. It wasn't even a clean knockdown. What it was was a whole lot of pain and confusion on my part. On their part it was not just one but two more applications of something hard against the side of my head.

They got their clean knockdown and their clean knockout.

Now you know and I know what they were after. There was absolutely no other reason to come after me the way they had. They didn't find it, because I had put the envelope back in the wall safe before I went to the john. The only person I was sure it hadn't been was the good senator himself. All he would have had to do was ask when he showed up for his appointment.

I went down the hall and got a good look at the lump on the side of my head. Ugly, but not bleeding. I leaned into the bathroom mirror to check my eyes. They looked normal, though I wasn't sure what I was looking for exactly.

I returned to my office, sat behind my desk, took out a pint of Jim Beam, and had a nice self-indulgent shot. Two shots, in fact. Jamie had left part of a can of Pepsi. I used the rest of it to gulp down two aspirins.

I was starting to calm down. I'd been scared and then mad and then scared-mad and now I was just mad. And puzzled. Why hadn't the senator shown up, and why had somebody come in his place?

Though you never hear much about them, both parties have political operatives who perform all kinds of services for their employers.

What a service it would be to hand over photos of the senator and his mistress to the man running against him. Now, no opponent would be stupid enough to call a press conference and share the photos with every leering reporter in the state. The opponent couldn't use the photos in any public way without implicating himself and looking seedy.

But there was certainly a way the photos could be used privately. This particular tactic had been used before. Opponent takes photos to the senator and demands that the senator withdraw, otherwise the photos will be circulated privately to reporters.

Some people can tolerate scandal. They can go before their public and apologize with wife and children by their side and go on from there. But there are those who can't, those who are willing to give up the power that comes with a Senate seat, rather than face a scandal-hungry press that will likely not let go of the subject for some time.

What the hell was going on here?

I ATE—don't ask me why in the Edward Hopper diner. Slice of peach pie, cup of coffee. As usual, the place was mostly empty. I was all things at once—tired, restless, angry, baffled.

I'd brought along my nickel notebook to make out the list I probably should have made out forty-eight hours ago.

Rob Anderson
Nick Hannity
Lucy Williams
Senator Williams
Will Neville
James Neville

Those were the primary suspects. The Neville brothers had to be included because they had a good reason to kill their little brother—to take over his black-mail business and find the cash he'd already amassed.

I also needed to make a separate list of those he'd been blackmailing, the names on the manila envelopes I'd handed out tonight. Last names only. I'd been able to guess correctly which family member bearing the name was being blackmailed. Logic and familiarity dictated a husband in one case and a wife in another, whereas the third had been determined by my favorite scientific method, the lucky guess.

"Your handwriting is worse than mine."

She slipped onto the counter stool next to me. Her perfume set off an alarm in my trousers.

"It was good enough for the nuns," I said.

"The nuns always gave boys the benefit of the doubt."

"That's not true."

"Sure it is. Think back. I went to Catholic school, too."

"Since when are Sykeses Catholics?"

"My dad saw this movie when he was in Italy during the war. You know, one of those corny things where there's a miracle in the end?"

"I always hated those movies. They always embar-rassed me."

"Me, too. But they didn't embarrass my dad. He wrote my mom that he wanted all of us baptized Catholic right away. He'd already been baptized. So, anyway, after seventh grade, I went to Catholic school. And the nuns preferred the boys."

I saw her looking at the list on my notebook page. I flipped the cover closed.

"I already saw it. I do the same. Make out a list of suspects."

The night man came and took her order for coffee and a piece of buttered toast.

"So how'd it go with Rob Anderson?"

"He now has a lawyer, and a damn good one. Frank Pierson. Des Moines."

"Yeah, he is good."

"Pierson allowed us half an hour and he did most of the talking. Anderson just sat there and smirked. God, he's a jerk."

"You ask him about the tar baby?"

"Of course. Pierson answered that one, too, and said that it was just a prank and that it hadn't even been constructed."

"Because he couldn't find anybody who'd do it for him."

"According to Pierson, even if it *had* been built, it wouldn't have any bearing on the case."

"I'd like to hear him try that one in court. You could take him apart with it."

"I did. In fact, that was the only point I scored. I said it spoke to state of mind and to motive—how much he hated Leeds."

"What'd Pierson say?"

"Said it was tangential and a waste of time."

"So I don't suppose you learned anything new?"

Her coffee and toast came. She ate fast. "Haven't had anything since lunch." Then she turned to me and said, "Even if I did learn something new, I can't share it with you, Sam. Remember?"

"Oh, right."

"So it's no fair asking me. I wouldn't want to damage our relationship."

"Some relationship."

She swallowed the last of her toast. "You know your problem?"

"No, but I'm sure you're going to tell me."

"You love being in love. A lot of people are like that. And it's fun. In the beginning, anyway. It's like you're high all the time. Everything is new and exciting—even though you've been through it with a number of people before—and it's like you're living in this state of grace. And that's what you're after."

"I probably am. So what's so wrong about that?"

"Nothing at all, Sam. I love that feeling, too. But I've been through too many ups and downs with men. For once in my life, I want to take my time. And you don't. You want the exhilaration immediately. Two dates and we're sleeping together and living in this Technicolor romance. And then in six or seven months it all falls apart."

I gave it some honest thought. Because the night man was listening so carefully, I almost asked him what *he* thought. Maybe we could have a vote and he'd be the tie-breaker.

"I'll tell you what. I think after the big heartbreak

of my life—a beautiful girl named Pamela Forrest—I think I probably was like that. But I don't think I'm like that anymore."

"You know what, Sam?" She rested her hand on my arm. "I was sort of the same way. Rush into things and then watch it all fall apart. So why don't we make a pact?" She glanced up at the night man. "How does that sound, sir? A pact?"

He smiled, wiped his hands on his grease-spotted apron. "I get up late in the mornings and my old lady always has soap operas on. This is just like one of those. A pact sounds great."

"Do I get to know what this pact is all about?"

"Why don't I tell you outside? We have some business to discuss, anyway."

As we were leaving, the night man said, "Stop back, you two, so I know how it works out."

We all laughed.

"WERE YOU EVER in that little wading pool over there, Sam?"

"Oh, sure."

"I'll bet you were cute."

"Skinny, that's for sure."

"I can picture you, actually."

We were sitting on the steps of the bandstand in the middle of the town square.

"So how about that pact, laddie?"

"Laddie?"

"I heard Maureen O'Hara say that on the late movie last night. If it's good enough for Maureen, it's good enough for me."

"Yeah, I mean, sure, the pact I mean. Slow and easy."

She put out her hand and we shook. We sat silent in the darkness then, watching a lonely dog sniff around the grounds and the teenagers roar by in their custom cars, radios blaring, Roy Orbison and Jan & Dean and Lesley Gore providing the soundtracks for all those high school lives that would make sense only years later to those who had lived them.

"Did you used to drive up and down the street like they do?"

"Sure."

"Did the beautiful Pamela Forrest ever go with you?"

"Sometimes, when she was mad at tall, dark, handsome, and very rich Stu."

"Her boyfriend?"

"Up several notches. Her god."

"I had one of those in high school. My girlfriends always said that when he was looking into my eyes, he was actually looking at his own reflection."

I smiled. "Maybe sadomasochism is the essence of all romantic love."

"As long as I get the 'sadist' part, I'll be happy." Then: "You ready for some business talk?"

"Sure. Because 'laddie' here is getting a little chilly."

"C'mon, then, you can walk me back to my hotel and we can talk along the way."

And talk we did.

"Did you talk to the judge today?"

"No. I tried to get in to see her but she still doesn't want to talk to me."

"She's going to the clinic in Minnesota."

"Yes. I'll drive her if she wants me to."

"I know how much you care about her. But since she's going there, it seems to me that we can go on with our original plan and work together."

"I've been thinking about that, too."

"Good. Have you also been thinking about who might have killed Leeds and Neville?"

"I keep going back and forth between Anderson and Hannity."

"So do I, actually. But I'm not one hundred percent sure about either of them. I've been thinking about the senator, in fact."

"The senator. He had the most to lose."

I'd been wondering if I should tell her about what had happened in my office tonight. I did.

"I didn't notice any bump on your head."

"It's gone down a lot."

"You don't think you should have it checked?"

"I'm fine."

"You know, in private-eye novels they take a lot of punishment. But in real life you can die from something like that."

"I'm fine. Really."

We stood a quarter of a block from her hotel, in the shadows of an old movie theater that had closed down.

I put out my hand. "Well, I guess we shake hands good-night, huh?"

"Oh, I think we can do better than that, laddie."

And we sure as hell did.

TWENTY-THREE

THE WINDOW WENT just after midnight. Two rocks the size of a heavyweight's fist, as I learned later.

Sitting up in bed. Real or nightmare, that glass-smashed sound?

The cats weren't sure, either. Usually they would've jumped off the bed. But they were as frozen as I was. Real or nightmare?

The third rock came through the window on the opposite side of the back door.

No doubt about this one.

The cats and I sprang off the bed. I found my slippers, wanting to avoid cutting the hell out of the bottoms of my feet, and rushed to the window for a look.

The backyard, limned by moonlight, shimmered summer-night beautiful in moon shadow and glistening dew. Even the two garbage cans looked like pieces of art in the darkness.

One of them peeked out from the alley side of the garage. Couldn't be sure but it looked like Hannity. But they would be operating as a team.

They were getting ready for another assault.

During the next three or four minutes I got into my jeans and penny loafers sans socks, then grabbed my dad's army .45 from the bureau and started my way down the interior steps of the house.

The widow Goldman waited for me at the bottom of the stairs. Even somewhat sleep-mussed, she was still a slightly better-looking version of Lauren Bacall. She had a blue silk robe drawn tight up to her neck. Everybody should have such a landlady, though that seemed too coarse a word for someone as stylish, bright, and gentle as Mrs. Goldman.

"Are you all right?"

"Fine."

"Let me call the police."

"No. Please don't."

"Good Lord, Sam. That's a gun in your hand."

"My dad's from the war."

"Please, Sam. Let me call the police. Let them settle this. In fact, why don't you stay down here with me. That way I know you won't do anything crazy."

"I know who it is, Mrs. Goldman. I can handle it."

"With a gun?"

"Just for show. Honest."

"Good Lord, Sam. A gun?"

"I'll stop by when I'm done with this."

Just then another window shattered upstairs.

"I'll make sure they pay for every one of them, Mrs. Goldman."

"Sam, it's you I'm worried about. Not somebody paying for the windows."

I didn't want to miss them. I opened the front door and said, "I'll be right back."

The night was exhilarating, rich in scents of newly

mown grass, loam, the wood of respectable old houses, and the cool air of the prairie.

I swung wide, running quickly up the street, then darting between houses and out to the alley.

I stood in the shadow of a garage overhang, watching them. They were gathering rocks for their next assault. Rob Anderson and Nick Hannity. America's youth.

I didn't have to worry about them seeing me. They were too drunk to see past their own hands.

I stayed in the shadows and started moving slowly down the alley. Anderson glanced up once. I thought he might have seen me. But I ducked behind a pile of fireplace logs and stayed there for a few minutes. If he'd seen me, he'd quickly forgotten about it.

I waited until their backs were turned away from me, until they were taking position to start throwing again. They were going to run out of windows soon.

"Drop the rocks. And hands up in the air."

Hannity started to twist around, but then I stepped into the moonlight and gave him a peek at my .45.

"Shit, man, what's the gun for?"

"Because I'm taking you in."

"It was Rob's idea, man. Not mine."

Now Rob turned around to face me. "That's bullshit. This was your idea, you jerk."

"Doesn't matter whose idea it was. You both smashed out windows. You both broke the law."

"My folks are gonna be so pissed it's unbelievable," Anderson said. His voice sounded reasonably sober. But the way he kept jerking around, trying to stay in one place without simply falling over, gave him away.

"Which one of you killed Leeds and Neville?"

"He did, man," Anderson said. "I was at a movie and I can prove it. He did. He was afraid Nancy Adams was going to sleep with the Negro."

"You lying bastard. You were afraid Lucy was gonna sleep with him!"

In their white T-shirts and jeans, they looked young and harmless. But there was a good chance they weren't harmless at all. There were a lot of racists in this country, but when you added the scorn of the upper classes to the scorn of race, you had a real monster.

"Step up here, Anderson."

"Why should I, you bastard? You don't mean shit to me."

"Because I'm going to cuff you."

"Handcuffs?"

"That's right." I'd brought two pairs, just in case. "Turn around. Hands behind your back."

I kicked him hard in the shin. He called me several names, at least two of which I'd never heard before. Every time he tried to move on me I shoved the .45 in his face. He still hadn't turned around.

Another shin kick worked wonders.

He turned around. He was crying. Unfortunately my pity function seemed to be turned off.

Hannity, being Hannity, had lunged at me twice while I was cuffing Anderson. Both times I'd shouted at him close up and put the gun in his face. He'd stepped back. I think the shout bothered him more than the gun.

"You're not gonna get me in those easy, McCain, I'll tell you that."

"Then you'll be going to jail with one hell of a headache."

He didn't expect it, but when it landed, I think he was as much shocked as hurt. And that wasn't right. So I hit him again, and this time I was sure he was more hurt than shocked. The way I'd intended.

He'd probably never been slugged on the temple with a gun before—come to think of it, neither had I—but he sure caught on fast about the protocol of it all. He staggered and touched his fingers to his head. I grabbed the other hand and used it to whip him around. I got one cuff on him and said, "You can either put your other hand around your back or you can get hit again and I'll do it for you."

Anderson was sobbing. Between the alcohol and the rage and the dim recognition that he was, yes indeed, going to jail, he was coming apart.

Hannity gave up the fight. He was no doubt plotting my death.

I got him cuffed, both hands.

Mrs. Goldman was gliding down the backyard walk. "Are you all right, Sam?"

"Would you be so kind as to call the police?"

"Of course. But are you all right?"

"I'm fine."

She turned back toward the house and hurried to her own rear door.

"You sleepin' with her, are you?" Hannity said.

"Yeah, as soon as I finish with your mother, I usually grab Mrs. Goldman."

"You don't know what's gonna happen to you, McCain. My old man's right. You're just trash from the Knolls. You've got it in for us because we've got money and you don't."

"Knolls trash is right. You little jerk. You just wait till my old man gets done with you." Anderson would've sounded meaner if he hadn't been crying while he threatened me.

When the cop car came, I helped pile them into the backseat, then I got in my ragtop and followed them to the station.

"'Lo."

"Don't bother to look at your clock. I'll tell you the time." Which she did.

"Jane."

"Uh-huh. I thought I'd share the misery with you."

"Oh, shit."

"At least."

"Anderson's old man and Hannity's old man. They called, I bet."

"Anderson's old man called. Hannity's old man came over."

"Oh, God."

"He plans to use all his power, which he seems to think is considerable, to get your law license lifted."

"God, I'm sorry."

"Don't be. You did the right thing. I mean, these two are spoiled brats to the highest power. I suppose he would've visited you, but then he would have had to look at all the windows they broke."

"The breeze is nice, but I don't appreciate all the bugs."

"But neither one called?"

"Yeah. But I hung up after they started calling me names."

"Well, expect trouble tomorrow. You'll be hearing from their lawyers. You don't have to be nice to them, but I have to, since I'm supposedly the objective third party."

"I still think those two jerks are good for the murders."

"So do I. Now more than ever, in fact. This shows how irrational they are. I'd love to get either one of them on the witness stand."

"Damn."

"What?"

"A bug. The cats are going crazy, chasing them all over the place."

"Good. Then you'll be as tired as I am in the morning."

"Yeah, but you'll look prettier than I do."

"Listen, Sam, you made some serious enemies tonight."

"I know."

"They don't have as much power as they think they do, but I'll bet their lawyers can get them a hearing on your license. I wouldn't make them any madder than you already have."

"I won't. Damn."

"Bug?"

"Yeah."

"'Night, Sam. Just remember what I said."

"I'm not likely to forget it. They'll be all over me tomorrow."

AT 9:30 THE NEXT MORNING I wandered around the flower shop looking for something appropriate to send to Jane. I wasn't sure what the occasion was—thanking her for waking me up in the middle of the night?—but I hadn't bought a woman flowers in quite some time and doing so always made me feel better about myself, as if I had a bit of class after all.

The siege had run about an hour, 8:00 a.m. to 9:00 a.m. First Mr. Anderson and then Mr. Hannity, full of threats, had called me about their sons. Then their lawyers called to tell me about all the things they were suing me for, both of them adding that I would be lucky to be a legal secretary this time next year. And then finally Nick Hannity himself called to tell me that he hadn't forgotten about last night. I congratulated him on his remarkable powers of recall.

Jamie sat there with tears in her eyes. She could hear some of them shouting at me. After each call she'd said, "He's such a mean SOB, Mr. C."

I, in turn, called the most successful lawyer I knew in Cedar Rapids, laid it all out for him and asked him to tell me if I was in any serious trouble. He said he didn't see how. He mentioned case law for every part of the incident and every one was in my favor. He told me to relax and to steer any further calls, messages, or bomb threats to his office.

"Why, good morning," Karen Porter said. "Well, maybe I shouldn't say 'good morning' after last night."

She was in her domain here, an attractive middle-aged widow who'd co-owned this florist business with Ellen Williams longer than the senator had held his seat in Washington. Her youthful face made her graying hair look out of place.

Walking into the store was like sliding down the

center of a bouquet of flowers, sights and scents overwhelming, the beauty and aromas almost alien in their
lushness, like those in a hundred pulp science fiction
stories I'd read, where the gorgeous forest finally
grabbed you and ate you, a light snack for the monsters
disguised as tulips.

"Ellen called me in the middle of the night. I'd never
heard her that upset before. She just kept sobbing and
sobbing and sobbing."

"Wasn't the senator there to help her?"

"You know Lloyd. As much as I love him, he's
useless in a crisis." She glanced around the store,
making certain that we were alone. "He just gets angry
and sputters and splutters. I almost feel sorry for him.
He just can't deal with crises."

"I wonder how Lucy's doing."

She frowned. "I'm a family friend. So I probably
shouldn't be kibitzing this way. But I think Lucy
could've thought the whole thing through a little better."

"'The whole thing' being David Leeds."

"I actually liked David. I had him do some work
around here. Best helper we ever had. Punctual, bright,
really hard-working. I was all for David and Lucy going
out. I just wish they could have confined it to Iowa City.
We've got a nice town here. Once most of us got over
the initial shock of Lucy and David being together, we
did our best to accept it. That doesn't mean to condone
it exactly but just to say that it was their own business.
And if people had opinions, they kept them private. They
were still nice to Lucy and still nice to David. But of
course there's always ten, twenty percent who can't
accept anything or anybody different. And they're active

about it. We lost a few customers here who didn't want David to wait on them because he was going out with Lucy. Can you imagine that? You look at people like that and you think they must be insane. They can't get past anything that's different." She leaned in, "Of course, the senator is like that himself. Anything a little bit different and he can't deal with it. Look at his voting record. The traditional way is the best way even if it doesn't work anymore." She smiled. "How was that for a speech?"

"I told you ten years ago you should run for mayor."

"Why, when Howie provides us with so much fun?"

Howard D. K. Fogerty Jr. was both the local Chrysler dealer and the mayor. He was given to quoting Herbert Hoover, a local boy who probably deserved better by historians than he'd received thus far. He also quoted, no kidding, the Lone Ranger. In his most memorable commencement speech, he'd quoted not just the masked man himself but also Tonto. The town was waiting for him to quote the Ranger's horse, Silver.

The bell above the shop door rang.

"Duty calls," she said, smelling wonderfully of an exotic perfume as she passed by me.

From flowers I can't tell you. I know what a rose looks like, a red one anyway, and I know what a gardenia looks like. The rest of them, I'm pretty shaky on.

I walked up and down the aisles. I was in no hurry to make my decision. I was glad to be out of the office for a while. Poor Jamie. She'd probably had a breakdown by now.

I stuck with the roses. By the time I hit the counter,

the store was busy. Karen Porter was waiting with a customer. I gave my order to one of the Klemson twins. Betty Klemson worked in the store here while Sandy Klemson had eloped with the Gutterman boy who'd since joined the navy. The now pregnant Sandy was living in San Diego with many other navy wives. Every once in a while I read the "Catching Up" column about former citizens of ours now living afar.

"Half dozen red roses, please." Then: "Wait a minute. Make that two orders of a half dozen roses each." Mrs. Goldman deserved a treat too. Thanks to me, she probably hadn't gotten much sleep last night.

"Sure, Mr. McCain."

I gave her Mrs. Goldman's name and address and then Jane's.

"Boy, she's a really classy woman, isn't she?"

For some reason I was suddenly back in ninth grade and sending roses to the beautiful Pamela Forrest, the sort of thing that was embarrassing to a he-man freshman.

Right there and right then, a grown man, a court investigator and a private eye, I did the unthinkable. I blushed.

OUTSIDE THE HOSPITAL ROOM where James Neville was currently residing, Cliffie had stationed one of his auxiliary cops, a scrawny kid named Sullivan who stood rather than sat in the chair they'd provided for him. Hard to look tough when you were sitting down. Leaning against the wall like this, your right hand on the handle of your holstered weapon, a suspicious squint for everybody who passed by in the hall, people knew you were tough. Except he'd spilled some coffee or cola on his tan cotton auxiliary police shirt and that detracted from his tough-guy pose. Tough guys should never be spillers.

"You got permission to go in there, McCain?" He hated me because Cliffie hated me. That was the first thing they learned under his tutelage. Cliffie good, Judge Whitney/Sam McCain bad.

"Do I *need* permission?"

"You do as far as I'm concerned."

"All I need is five minutes."

"That ain't what the chief said."

"How about the district attorney?"

"Who?"

"Cliffie's cousin."

"You ain't supposed to call him Cliffie."

"Well, she's technically his boss. And she gave me permission."

"Is that true?"

"Which part?"

"Her bein' his boss?"

"That's how I learned it in law school."

Like hell I did.

"And she really gave you permission?"

"She did indeed."

He looked around. I didn't feel good about lying to him. Sullivan was stupid but he wasn't mean. He just liked to play dress-up like most of the other auxiliary cops. I'd seen him playing cop at the county fair and the Fourth of July corn roast. He was nice to everybody. Why couldn't he be one of Cliffie's thugs? Then I wouldn't feel so guilty about getting him in trouble with Cliffie.

But then I remembered the promise I'd made to Cy out there on his porch.

"Five minutes is all and if Clifford says anything to you, tell him to call me and I'll take complete responsibility."

"You will?"

"I will."

"Say, you wouldn't happen to have any gum on you, would you?"

"Two sticks or three?"

"Two'd do fine. I got a break comin' up here."

While he was unwrapping the first stick, I made my way inside the room where Will Neville sat on a chair talking to his brother James, who lay in the bed with his right arm in a cast and enough gauze and tape on the rest of him to wrap up Boris Karloff in a *Mummy* sequel.

"You get that son of a bitch out of here," James said. "I wouldn't be in here except for him." James grimaced. He was in pain of some sort.

Will got up. He was going to lumber over to me and pound my head in. I reached in my back pocket and brought forth my sap. "This can put you in a bed right next to James here, Will. I'd think it over."

"You son of a bitch."

"I think James already said that, Will."

"You got no business here."

James grimaced again.

"Boys," I said. "I'm here to find out who killed your brother. And I expect you to help me find out. Otherwise, James, you're going to go straight from the hospital here to a jail cell. Personally, I'd prefer the hospital. You don't get all those cute nurses in jail."

"What the hell's he talking about, James?"

"Yeah, McCain, what the hell are you talking about?"

I lit a Lucky Strike. "You ran some kind of blackmail ring in Chicago. You told Richie how to set one up here. That comes under the heading of felony, in case you forgot all the law you learned while you were in Joliet."

Will looked at James, then at me. "You can't prove that."

"Well, among all the rubble at the murder scene, I found several pieces of equipment in the darkroom that had been bought in Chicago. Sounds like you bought him one of those handy-dandy blackmail kits, huh?"

"You can't prove that," Will said again.

This was where I decided to risk another lie. Two a day is usually my limit, but this was a sudden-death playoff and I needed it bad.

"I haven't figured out your share of the proceeds yet, but after Richie made his collections—once a month, I suspect—he sent you your cut. Fine and dandy, but he did it by check."

Both their faces froze as what I'd just said registered in their small criminal minds.

"So any smart detective and any smart DA could lay their hands on bank records and demonstrate the pattern of payout you and Richie had going."

I pulled up a chair and sat down. "If you think I'm lying about any of this, wait and see how fast I can have a detective up here."

"A detective from Cliffie's office?" Will sneered.

"Even a detective from Cliffie's office could figure this one out. And even if he can't, the DA can."

"I hear you're trying to get into her panties," Will said.

"And I hear you don't wear any panties, Will."

And the troops arrived. A doc and two nurses. They swept in as if they had been dispatched by Divine Providence. One of the nurses pushed a wheelchair.

The doc didn't deign to look at me or Will. To James, he said, "I'm afraid we'll have to run some more tests on you, Mr. Neville."

"When can I get the catheter out?" James said. No wonder he'd been grimacing.

Will glanced at me and said sotto voce, "That's got to hurt." And then he pointed to his crotch in case I hadn't heard.

Both nurses scowled in Will's direction.

"I'll wait out in the hall," I said.

Nobody was crying, there were no code blues, nobody was wheeled past in the last stages of their lives. The three or four times I'd been in the hospital I'd enjoyed myself. When I was a small boy, I got Green Lantern and Captain Marvel comic books. And when I was older, I got the names and phone numbers of several nursing students who later proved to be damn good dates.

But as the years pass, hospital visits start to get grim. No more bad tonsils and busted legs from sliding into second in the kids' league. Now you're into the real business of hospitals: hushing up and sanitizing the process of death. But every once in a while all the hushing-up fails and you get a glimpse of a frightened doctor or the knife-sharp sob of a loved one or the stark stink of bowels bursting at the point of death itself.

The irony of standing in a hospital hall smoking a cigarette, after several years of the surgeon general pounding home the connection between cancer and heart attack and cigarettes, wasn't lost on me. If I ever managed to get married and have kids, would they be standing in this very hall twenty, thirty years down the line wishing that the old man in the room behind them had never taken up the devil weed?

The nurse pushed the wheelchair carrying James Neville out of the room and down the hall. Then came the doc and the other nurse. Both heading to the elevator, too. No sign yet of Will.

When I entered the room, he was standing by the window, looking down at the activity in the parking lot.

"I know you think we're dumb," he said, knowing who was there without turning around. "But that don't mean it hurts any less."

"Richie?"

"He was a good kid."

"Then help me catch his killer."

He swung his large head around and looked at me. "Can't. We say anything it's like confessing we were in on it."

"I wouldn't have to tell anybody what you told me."

"James says you're a liar. I say you are, too."

"I guess I won't be getting invited to your family reunion, huh?"

"I get sick of your jokes."

"I get sick of them sometimes, too. But what makes me real sick is somebody getting away with murder. A lot of crimes go unsolved, you know."

"Not murder."

"You're wrong, Will. Lots of murders go unsolved.

The cops call them 'open files.' But 'open' really means the opposite. 'Closed.' They give up on them."

"Maybe in the big city."

I lit another smoke. "Remember when the two Furnish girls were found beaten to death in the woods? All the publicity that got? They still haven't found the killer."

He looked back at the parking lot below.

"You and your brother had a lot of responsibility here, Will. It was you two who got him into this black-mail thing and you damn well know it. He'd be alive today if it wasn't for you two."

"Shut your face."

"James runs the same kind of setup in Chicago and then he brings it out here to Richie. Sort of like a fran-chise. Like the Dairy Queen or something."

We didn't talk for a while.

"I need to know if anybody hassled Richie over being blackmailed. Did anybody get mad? Did anybody try to hurt him? Did anybody threaten to go to the law? You're running out of chances here, Will. I gave you a chance to talk while I was at your apartment. Now I'm giving you another chance."

"You don't give a shit about Richie. You just want to find out who killed him—for your own sake."

"You're being real stupid here, Will. Real stupid. You've already lost a brother. Maybe you and James will lose your freedom, too. Going to prison."

There was nothing more to say. I stood there staring at his back for a few more seconds and then I left.

WHEN I GOT TO the ground floor, I found an open phone booth and called the judge's house. A year ago her longtime employee had decided to retire to Florida and in his place she now had a chauffeur/functionary who seemed to think he was also her press secretary. Stingy he was with info, Aaron Towne.

"How's she doing?"

"Just about how you'd think she'd be doing."

"Well, at least she was able to go home. I imagine the master bedroom looks like a hospital room."

"We've been able to make it serve her needs."

"You know something, Aaron?"

"I'm not sure I appreciate that tone."

"Well, I don't really give a shit what you appreciate or not. She's not only my boss, she's my friend."

"If you're such a good friend of hers, why did she give me specific instructions not to bring her your calls or let you in the door?"

"Because she's embarrassed, that's why. Because she's lonely and afraid and ashamed and she needs to talk to me more than ever."

"Well, she won't talk to you. And I won't ask her to. She spends way too much time worrying about you as it is."

"What? She worries about me?"

"She worries that you'll never really get ahead as a lawyer. She worries that you resent the important people in this town to the point where it holds you back. And she worries that you'll be as unhappy in love as she's been."

Four husbands. At least she knew whereof she spoke.

"I see."

"So right now seeing her would be unwise—both for you and for her."

But right now I wasn't listening all that carefully. I was thinking of that imperious, elegant middle-aged woman worrying about me. I'd never had much of a hint that she considered me any more important to her than the milkman. Probably less, because she really liked milk.

"Please give her a message for me, Aaron."

"If it's the right kind of message."

"Tell her that I'm really eager to see her and that she's in my thoughts and prayers constantly."

"I guess I could tell her that."

"You're such a swell guy, Aaron."

"I know you're being sarcastic, McCain."

"Gosh," I said, "how could you tell?"

TWENTY-FOUR

I WAS DOING MY Philip Marlowe routine—feet up on the desk, pipe in my mouth, copy of Mr. Hefner's latest fitting nicely between my hands—when he appeared in my doorway. This was just after five. Jamie had gone home and the office was quiet, especially since I'd taken the phone off the hook.

"I didn't realize you were an intellectual," Senator Williams said, nodding at the magazine.

"I've looked at all the pictures several times. Now I'm actually reading it."

"I'm told they do have a good article or two on occasion." He walked in and said, "Mind if I sit down?"

"Of course not."

I'd never seen him this dressed down. Button-down yellow shirt, brown belt, brown slacks. His hair was wind-mussed, too. He'd almost lost that senatorial pose he lived inside.

He seemed to be as nervous as I was about his visit. I wasn't sure what he wanted.

"Thanks for dropping those negatives off at my office today. I'm sorry I didn't make it last night."

"That's fine. I survived. So what can I help you with today?"

"I need to ask you something, Sam."

"All right."

"Are you sure those were the only negatives you had with my name on the envelope?"

"Sure. I gave you everything I had."

"And you didn't look at them?"

"No, I didn't. I kept my word."

He started leaning forward, sliding his hand behind him, apparently to retrieve his wallet.

"I have money, Sam. Plenty of money. I'm sure Esme doesn't pay you all the money in the world."

"Why are you offering me money?"

He paused and then said, "We're sort of talking in code here."

"We are?"

"Look, Sam. I know you held the rest of those negatives back. Make a little money for yourself. I don't blame you. You're the one who's really done most of the work on this matter. But now I need the rest of the negatives." This time he succeeded in getting his wallet out. "I brought plenty of money, Sam. So let's talk about me getting the rest of the negatives and you getting the seven hundred dollars in my wallet here."

"Don't bother with any money. First of all, I wouldn't want it even if I had the negatives—"

Anger in those cold, disapproving eyes. He had restrained himself as long as he could. "Even if you had the negatives? Where the hell are they?"

"I don't know what negatives you're talking about."

He sat back in his chair, folded his hands in his lap, and just stared at me. His lips were white and his eyes moments from expressing the rage I could feel even across the desk.

"You really expect me to believe this bullshit?"

"And what bullshit would that be?"

"You're as bad as Neville. And since you're smarter than he was, your price will probably be higher, too."

"You think I'm shaking you down for the negatives?"

"What the hell else would you be doing?"

"Get the hell out of here."

"What?"

"You heard what I said. I'm not putting up with this crap. I don't shake people down. And I don't have the negatives you're talking about."

"Then where the hell are they?"

Then: "Oh, shit." He rubbed his face. I was pretty sure I heard him sob. He dropped his hand. "Listen, I owe you an apology."

"Yeah, you do."

"You'd be as overwrought as I am if you were in my spot."

"Maybe. But I'd be a lot more careful of making accusations."

He sighed. Rubbed his face again.

"So you don't have any idea where they are?"

"If I did, I'd go get them."

"Yes, I suppose you would."

He snapped up from his chair and walked over to the window. "There're spies everywhere." Then he turned to me and smiled. "How paranoid does that sound?"

"I imagine it's true."

"My worthy opponent's got just as many gumshoes and political ops on me as I have on him."

"You think it was one of them who slugged me?"

"I'd say it was a good possibility, wouldn't you?"

"Maybe."

He came back and sat down. That sudden explosion of energy had seemed to drain him.

"I can still win. If we can get those negatives back before they get to the wrong people."

"How's Lucy?"

He looked shocked that I'd brought her up. My God, we were talking about his career and I'd had the nerve to drag in something as trivial as his daughter's well-being?

He waved me off. "Oh, you know, still moping. She's like her mother. Everything's my fault. Now her mother's telling me if I'd been a more 'loving' father maybe Lucy wouldn't be so—disturbed." He made a face. "'Disturbed' is the code word. There's some clinical insanity on my wife's side of the family. Dementia in two of her sisters. I think we may be looking at something clinical with Lucy. Not as severe as dementia but certainly some kind of serious dys-function mentally."

So who could blame *him* if his daughter's misery was genetic? He was blameless as always.

He stood up. He seemed lost, not quite sure where he was. "I thought it'd be so easy. I'd just come down here and get the negatives tonight. I thought I'd be all done with this. But it's still going on, isn't it?"

He went to the door. "If you find any more negatives, call me right away, Sam. Please. I'll pay you anything for them. Anything you ask."

"If I find any more negatives pertaining to you, I'll hand them over to you. No charge. Again, I'm not in the shakedown business."

He stared out into the hallway. "It used to be so damned easy for me, Sam. Everything was. But not anymore. Not anymore." He sounded ghostly.

And then, head bent like a penitent's, he slowly left the building.

I sat there for a few minutes wondering what was going on. Certainly something was. Williams was terrified of negatives that weren't in his file. I doubted that the pictures he was after had to do with his adulterous affair. Presumably, those were the ones I'd given him.

What other kind of photos would shake him up this badly? I spent twenty minutes trying to finish off some paperwork. But concentration came hard. Too hard.

Preparing my papers for tomorrow was easier than reading briefs. I shoved papers into appropriate file folders and shoved the file folders into my briefcase.

I finally hung up the receiver and the phone rang instantly.

Jane said, breathlessly: "I was just about ready to come over there and get you. Get over to the hospital right away."

"What's wrong?"

"Somebody snuck into James Neville's room and killed him."

TWENTY-FIVE

FLASHING EMERGENCY lights imbued the three-story brick building with a blanched red hue. Cops were stationed at both side doors, two at the front. A crowd had already gathered. Some of them were probably visitors on their way home when all the alarms went off.

The cops recognized me and waved me through. I took the interior stairs rather than the elevator. I never ride when I can walk. There's something coffinlike about elevators that has always scared me a little.

The west wing of the third floor was in chaos. There was a sense that this part of the hospital had been invaded.

Patients were being wheeled out of their rooms and steered to the east wing. The police business would go on for hours. Not exactly a relaxing atmosphere for people recovering from gall bladder surgery or even more deadly operations.

Nurses, a pair of doctors, and a janitor were being interviewed by one of Jane's young assistants. She'd increased her staff by three.

The hospital boss stood off by himself. This was Public Relations Nightmare numbers 1—20. A murder in your hospital while a police officer was ostensibly standing guard. The hospital would recover, of course, but not before there was a trial in the press and an endless number of local jokes. His soft, round face gave the impression that he had been shunned by the entire human race.

Jane wore a pair of walking shorts and a white blouse. Her hair was done in a chignon, which provided an interesting contrast with the informality of her attire. She was talking with Cliffie and it was pretty clear, even though she was doing her best to make it appear that she was just having a conversation, that she was helping him set up the crime scene properly. She had walked all his cops through three nights of evidence-gathering. I'm told they weren't happy that they hadn't gotten overtime pay for sitting in the borrowed public school classroom. She'd even brought in two experts from the State Bureau of Investigation. For joy for joy.

But her diligence looked to be working. I'd never seen Cliffie's men working a crime scene so efficiently.

Jane came over. "The man standing guard went to the bathroom. If he's telling the truth, he was gone no more than five minutes."

"So somebody was watching him, waiting to make a move."

"It appears that way."

"Anybody see anybody else going into or out of the room?"

"The only people working this wing are the two docs, the nurse, and the janitor my people are interviewing now. And they didn't see anybody."

"How'd he die?"

"Throat cut. The nurse on duty said that Neville had been given a heavy sedative about half an hour ago.

He'd had trouble sleeping. So he probably wasn't in any shape to resist, especially with a broken arm."

"Anybody call his brother Will?"

"Busy signal. I should check it again."

"Let me do it."

She watched my face as if it was going to reveal something to her.

"You wouldn't forget our little bargain, would you? About being partners?"

I hadn't thought about it since getting caught up in all the confusion up here. "Maybe I should tell you about Senator Williams dropping by."

"Yeah, Sam, maybe you should." The tone was impish; the eyes were remorseless.

So I told her, finishing up with, "I have no idea what the negatives are."

"But he was really upset."

"Very upset. Like he was dazed or something. He seems to think that his whole career is on the line here."

"That's strange. He got the negatives you said he'd wanted in the first place—"

Just then one of her assistants waved her over.

"I'd better check on this. Are you going to try Neville's phone again?"

"Yeah. And if it's still busy, I may wander over there."

"You sure you're telling me everything?"

"You want me to swear on my ragtop that I'm telling you the truth?"

The imp again. "Sometime when we're just relaxing I want to talk to you about that car of yours. You ever think it's a little bit 'youthful' for a grown-up attorney?"

"'Youthful.' People generally aren't that kind."

"I need to go." And she was gone.

I walked down to the lobby, got a cup of coffee from the snack bar, headed over to the pay phone.

I had to look up his number. I got a busy signal for my trouble. I decided to make sure he hadn't just taken it off the hook, the way I had.

When I gave the operator my request, she said, "Is this an emergency, sir?"

"It could be. Does it matter?"

"We generally don't like to try the line this way unless it's an emergency. The teenagers ruined it for all of us. The girls, especially. They talk to each other for hours and their boyfriends can't get through. So the boyfriends start calling us to check on the line."

"I'd really appreciate it if you'd do this for me. It really could be an emergency."

"Well, I appreciate you being so courteous with me. You should hear some of those teenage boys."

There was a busy signal and then she said, "Please give me a minute. I have to check this now another way."

A busy signal for ten, fifteen seconds, then no sound at all.

"I can report this if you want me to."

"So the phone is off the hook?"

"That's what it appears. Would you like me to report it?"

"No, thanks. I appreciate your help."

The traffic was heavy tonight on the route I took to Will Neville's place. When I got there, I parked halfway down the block. A red ragtop is pretty easy to spot.

I walked between a sandwich shop and a vacuum cleaner repair shop to reach the alley. I wanted to come up the back way. If Will Neville had anything to hide, he'd hide it the moment he saw me coming up his sidewalk.

His car was there but the windows were dark on the second floor of the stucco house. Not even the moonlight could cast any magic on the debris that littered the backyard, including a tricycle without a front wheel, torn clothes, and pages of newspapers and magazines. Home sweet home.

I reached the stairs and started climbing. With each step, I knew I was drawing closer to something I didn't want to see.

TWENTY-SIX

WILL NEVILLE LAY facedown in the middle of his living room. There was enough moonlight through the nearest window to see that he was bleeding badly from a wound on the back of his head and I could see his back expand ever so subtly with each breath.

The place wasn't much messier than it had been when I'd visited here the other day. But still I could see, here and there, where it had been ransacked in a desperate search for something. And of course I knew what that something was.

I righted a floor lamp that had been knocked over, clipped on the light. In the bathroom I ran water into a grimy glass, grabbed a dirty bath towel, and went out to see what I could do for Neville.

I didn't try to get him to his feet. I just eased him up enough so that his back would rest against the front of the couch. I asked him a few questions. He answered only in moans. I put the glass to his lips. He didn't seem to understand the implications of it all. I said "Drink" and he said "Huh?"

As he drank, I dragged the floor lamp over for a closer look at his wound. The size of it startled me. Probably about that of a silver dollar.

I poured a slug of water onto the towel and started

to dab the wound. He let go with an uninterrupted thirty seconds of dirty words.

He spoke coherently for the first time: "Son of a bitch thinks he can get away with it because he's some big shot in Washington."

"Senator Williams?"

"You damn right Senator Williams. Big-shot asshole."

"He wanted those negatives?"

"Yeah." He grimaced and grabbed the towel from me. He was his old shitty self again. "But he didn't get 'em."

"How do you know? He knocked you out."

"Because I hid 'em where he'll never find 'em. Where nobody ever will. And they ain't just negatives. I got a set of photos of them too."

I stood up.

"Somebody killed your brother James about an hour ago."

He brought his head up too fast. He grabbed his head, the pain was so bad.

"In his hospital room. Somebody snuck in there and killed him."

"They couldn't have. Cliffie put a guard on that room. I seen them guards for myself. They rotated them around the clock."

"This guard went to the john and somebody got inside long enough to do the job. They cut his throat."

"Williams. That son of a bitch Williams. I bet it was him."

"Why would he kill James?"

"Because he musta thought James would tell him

where them negatives were. He probably thought I was too dumb to be in on it with Richie and James. But I been workin' with 'em three years."

"Three years? You three haven't been here three years."

"Different places."

I said, carefully, "I need to know where those photos are."

He looked like a giant baby sitting on the floor that way. He smiled up at me with that malicious homely face and said, "Well, I ain't telling ya."

"It's all over, Will. For all of you. You've got two brothers dead and you're headed for prison."

"Not with what I got, I ain't headin' to no prison." He smirked then grimaced again. "Senator Williams is gonna keep me out of prison."

"He can't. Not even a senator has that kind of power."

"Yeah, well, you ain't seen these pictures."

I suppose I could have given him a few more minutes. But I was tired of him and tired of the kind of game he and his brothers ran and so, almost without realizing what I was doing, I slipped my .45 from the pocket of my windbreaker.

He started to say something, but I brought my hand down so quickly that he didn't have time to get three words out.

I made sure that the barrel of the gun struck him right on the wound. And for good measure, I kicked him in the chest. And when he reared up, looking capable suddenly of pushing on through his pain, I kicked him in the chest again.

He fell back against the couch and started crying. I

think it was more frustration and hurt pride than pain. All his life he had been able to deal with problems by a force few could equal. But he'd been injured tonight and now I'd only made that injury worse. And for a humiliating moment here, a much smaller man was able to contain his wrath and his power.

His massive hand reached out to grab my leg and spill me, but his hand came in low and so I was able to stomp it to the floor with my heel. Bone cracked. This time his cry was more pain than wounded pride.

"I need to know where the photos are, Will. You might get lucky and grab me, but before that happens I'm going to keep on breaking your bones."

I whipped the gun barrel into his head wound again. For a time there he sounded inconsolable, just moaning, sobbing, moaning. Then he vomited all over his lap.

The smell didn't make his hovel any pleasanter.

I went over and sat on the edge of a chair across from him and said, "If you try to get up, I'll shoot you. I won't kill you but I'll put a bullet in your knee so you'll never walk right again. You understand me, Will?"

His head came up. His eyes and nose were gleaming messes and he had a chunk of vomit hanging from his chin.

I stood up and walked over to the phone and dialed the police station.

"Police station. Patrolman Emmett Billings."

Jane had improved the phone etiquette, too.

"Emmett, this is Sam McCain. I'm going to give you an address. I need a car here as fast as possible. I have a prisoner for you. Jane Sykes will explain this later."

He wouldn't have done it for me. But for the new district attorney, you bet.

I gave him the address. "Right away, Emmett. Please."

After I hung up, I walked back to Will Neville.

He was quiet now. He didn't smell any better. There was a dumb animal sorrow about him I couldn't enjoy anymore.

"I'm sorry I got so rough, Will."

"Yeah, I bet."

"If I tell the DA that you cooperated with me, I think I can get her to go easy on a few of the charges."

"She's Sykes's kin. She won't listen to you."

"She will in this case. We've been working together on it."

He raised his head two inches. Apparently, the pain was too much to bring it any higher.

"I done time in juvie. I don't want to go to no prison."

"You're not listening, Will. You'll probably have to do some time. But maybe I can cut some for you. That's what I'm talking about here."

"He could get me out of it entire."

"If you mean Williams, no, he couldn't. That's a pipe dream, Will. I'm offering you the only real kind of help that's available to you. Now tell me where those photos are."

And I'll be damned, right then and right there, if he didn't.

TWENTY-SEVEN

THE MAID SAID, "They're all in the library." She looked unhappily at the manila envelope in my right hand. "I hope that's not bad news. I don't think they could handle much more of it."

"Who's here?"

"The senator and his wife and daughter. Were you expecting somebody else?"

"No, I was just wondering."

The expression on her prim face now became suspicion. "I take it it is more bad news, then."

"I can't really talk about it."

"This whole house is coming apart."

"I'm sorry."

"So am I. I like it here, at least when the senator's out of town." Then: "I shouldn't have said that."

"I'm ready for the library anytime you are."

I followed her through the house. The living room was so brightly lit, it seemed a party was about to begin as soon as the guests swept up the drive in their cars—a night of pleasure for sure.

The maid knocked curtly. The conversation stopped. The senator said: "Yes, Marjorie?"

"Mr. McCain is here to see you."

"McCain—" He sounded confused.

"Excuse me," I said, as I covered the doorknob with my hand and pushed inward where the entire Williams family sat around a small table staring at me like the interloper I was. I had interrupted the most sacred business of all, private family business.

I walked in. The maid did me the favor of closing the door behind me.

"You weren't invited," Senator Williams said. "And I don't want you here."

"God, Dad," Lucy said. "That's so embarrassing, treating him like that."

"Lucy, why don't you pour him some coffee?" Ellen said.

"That sounds good about now."

The senator didn't try to hide his disgust with me. In fact, he made sure I'd see it by making faces and sighing deeply and shaking his head as I sat down. He seemed to think that I'd brought some kind of plague with me. As, perhaps, I had.

Lucy, dressed in a white T-shirt and jeans, poured me a cup of coffee from a carafe. "Sugar or cream?"

"Just plain is fine."

Each of them took turns staring at the manila envelope I'd set on the mahogany table in front of me.

The coffee was good. I took several sips of it in the uneasy silence. Then I finally said, "Any particular reason for this particular meeting?"

Lucy smirked. "We're each confessing our sins here, asking each other for forgiveness. And take my word for it, Mr. McCain, there's a lot to forgive."

"Haven't you done enough already? Why don't you

give it a rest? He's enjoying this. He'll tell everybody what a trashy family we are."

"Then he'll be telling the truth, won't he?" Ellen snapped.

The senatorial mask faded momentarily, replaced by a glimpse of weariness and dread. "Everything I've worked so hard to build, you two have tried to destroy. But by God, I'm not going to let you."

He knew what was in the envelope. That explained his unease. He'd lied to me about having an affair to cover up the real nature of the photos—his wife in bed with her business partner Karen. These were the photos he'd been desperate to keep from circulation. I really hadn't wanted to peek inside, but I hadn't had any choice. Unlike the other envelopes, this one had a bearing on a murder case.

"Maybe he's here to arrest one of us," Ellen said tartly. "That would be the final scandal, wouldn't it? Seeing your wife or your daughter in prison?"

"That was a consideration for a long time," I said. "You each had reasons for killing Leeds and Neville."

"Please don't talk about them in the same breath," Lucy said. "David was only trying to help us get"—she glanced at her mother—"get certain photos back from Neville. He was just trying to help us."

"A beautiful young white girl—*that's* why he was hanging around you, Lucy," her father said. "Goddammit, I wish you could understand that. He wanted a trophy. You've idealized him to the point where he—"

"He paid attention to her, he was proud of her, he genuinely loved her." Ellen's voice was hard, unforgiving. "Things you wouldn't know anything about, Senator."

"Knock off that 'Senator' bullshit. You know I hate that. I'm your husband."

"In name only."

"Maybe in name only to you. But not to me."

"Welcome to our little home, Mr. McCain," Lucy said. "And this is one of our *better* moments."

I tapped the manila envelope. I'd had enough of their family troubles. "So you told David about these photos?"

"Yes, and he kept our secret about Mom, too. I'm sure of it. He didn't tell anybody. David thought maybe he could reason with Richie. That's why he was there. Whoever killed Neville had to kill David so there wouldn't be any witnesses."

"That's what I was beginning to think, too," I said. Then, to the senator I said: "You never did have an affair, did you?"

"No."

"You only told me that so I wouldn't know what the photos were really about."

"I—didn't want the real truth to get out." He scowled at his wife. "The public might understand that I couldn't control my daughter if she wanted to go out with a Negro. But my wife being a sexual deviate—"

"Oh, God, Senator," Ellen snapped. "'A sexual deviate.' It happened twice."

I said, "Richie Neville had been trailing the senator. Trying to get something on him. A big payday if he could. But that wasn't going anywhere, so he decided to trail you for a while. That's how he found out about you and Karen. He did his Peeping Tom routine and got some photos of you in a bedroom together."

I shoved the envelope to her. "It's all yours. The negatives are in there, too."

"I sure as hell don't want them, McCain," Ellen said. "I'm not ashamed of what I did. Karen is my best friend. It was an act of affection more than anything. But these photos—they just make the whole thing dirty."

The senator stood up. "The whole thing was dirty. Is dirty. It's perverted and it's sickening."

"Do you feel the same way about all your girlfriends in Washington, Daddy?" Lucy said. "You're always in the gossip columns there. They never use your name but we know who they mean."

"That's completely different. At least it's—normal."

"I've had enough of this," Ellen said. And without warning fled to the door and vanished. Lucy was close behind her.

The senator sighed, ran a hand through his Hollywood hair. "At least it's over. I can deal with them privately. This won't affect the campaign."

I wanted to be astonished by his words, but I wasn't. I supposed that was another sign of growing up—albeit a bad one—that you moved beyond shock when you saw something truly ugly. You just accepted that it was there and then decided what to do about it.

"It isn't over, Senator."

He was the one who was astonished. He looked at me in disbelief. In the moments after his wife and daughter had left the room he'd managed to convince himself that everything was fine again.

"It isn't?"

"You beat up Will Neville pretty bad tonight."

"He didn't have it coming?"

"He's in police custody right now."

The dark eyes narrowed. He was beginning to understand what I was about to say. A part of it, anyway.

"Will is going to tell them everything he can to stay out of prison. You need to get to him before that happens."

"He's a blackmailer."

"He's a blackmailer who can take you down with him."

"Why are you trying to help me? You hate my politics and I'm sure you hate me."

"Because if you lose—and I hope you do—I want it to be because you're a shill for every crooked big businessman in the country. But I don't want to see you lose because of blackmail." Then: "Call your favorite local lawyer and get him to the hospital fast. I asked that he be looked at. He was in bad shape. Get him before Cliffie starts asking him any serious questions. Then you can bribe him or whatever it takes to keep him quiet about the blackmail photos. I scared him. I told him he was going to prison. You can tell him he isn't— if he'll do what you tell him. He'll be so relieved, he'll go along with anything you say."

"I trust everything that was said here tonight—"

"I like Lucy too much to say anything to anybody. And for the first time in my life, I like your wife. I think this experience gave her some humility, even if you'll never understand it that way."

He smiled. "And me—"

"You're just another whore for the robber barons. They're training your replacement now. If you win this time, it'll be your last term."

Anger filled the dark eyes. "I never realized until right this minute how much I detest you, McCain."

I tapped my chest. "Badge of honor, Senator. Badge of honor."

And that was where I left him.

I walked out to the ragtop and turned the key in the ignition. A blast of Chuck Berry. A cleansing blast of Chuck Berry. One I needed badly.

TWENTY-EIGHT

I SAW STAN GREEN'S Studebaker parked at the A&W on my way back to my office so I wheeled in, ordered myself a tenderloin and fries, and then walked over to Stan's car while I waited for my food to be deposited on the window ledge of my own car.

There was a time when the Studebaker with its futuristic grill and futuristic taillights looked downright…futuristic. Now it just looked sort of weird, like a sad mutant version of a real car.

"Still headed for outer space, I see."

"Oh, yeah," Stan said. "Headed for Mercury tonight. All those blue-skinned Mercurian babes."

Stan and I used to buy a magazine called *Planet Stories*. Sure, the half-naked women were green and mauve and blue sometimes, but they had breasts and hips that appealed to every boy who'd ever locked himself in his room with a magazine. The stories themselves were as ridiculously splendid as the sexy blue babes on the covers.

"Anything new for an intrepid reporter?"

"Not at the moment. Sorry."

"I still like Anderson and Hannity for it, don't you?"

"Pretty much."

He ate the last piece of his cheeseburger. I knew it

was a cheeseburger because he had dollops of melted cheese on his tie. The blue-skinned people who lived on Mercury had a strict dress code. Those cheese stains might get him barred.

At this time of night, just after nine-thirty, the testosterone parade was at its peak. There were the tough guys who walked around with the sleeves of their T-shirts rolled up so you could see their muscles. There were the boys in the cars with the glass-pack mufflers that could shake an entire building when the boys floored the gas pedals. And there were the lover boys, the ones all the carhops smiled at and sort of aimed their cute little bottoms at, the lover boys being too cool to acknowledge this in any way but all the other boys knowing that these bastards could have their pick of any carhop they wanted. And there were some sweet sweet carhops.

"I talked to Marie Denham tonight," Stan said.

"What about her?"

"She's getting discouraged. Wonders if the police are working as hard as they would if David had been white."

"Well, I admit everything's pretty confusing right now. Especially since somebody killed James Neville."

"Yeah, she said she's surprised nobody's arrested Will Neville. She said he's already violated his probation."

I saw the carhop bringing my food. "Well, just tell her we're doing our best. I don't blame her for being frustrated. We all are."

I finished my meal listening to Miles Davis on the Iowa City jazz station. The bleakness of his horn probably wasn't what I needed right then but it was too cool and too perfect to turn off.

I was thinking of something Stan had just said—or trying to remember what Stan had just said, something that had bothered me afterward—when I saw him back out of his slot and exit the root beer stand.

But the yawn that made me lay my head back against the seat put curiosity out of my mind. Not being a tough guy, and not being a guy who can get by on little sleep, the past few days of violence and quick naps were starting to sink me.

I'd been planning on going to my office, but right now that six-block trip seemed far too long. There was a phone booth on the west corner of the A&W. I'd check my messages from there and then head on home.

"Hi, it's McCain. Any messages?"

"One. Aaron Towne. He said you'd know the number."

"Thanks."

"For what it's worth, he wasn't very nice."

"He never is. I'm sorry, Julie."

"I'm the one who's sorry—for you."

Aaron answered and as soon as he realized who it was, he said, "You took your own sweet time."

"Aaron, now's not a good time to push it. Believe me. Now what the hell's going on?"

"She's decided she wants to go there tonight. She doesn't want anybody to see us leave town."

"I'm just glad she's going."

"She wants to talk to you."

"She's been avoiding me."

"If I had my way, she'd still be avoiding you. I don't

see where this will help her at all. But I'll go tell her. She'll pick up from the den. She's making lists of things for me to do."

"Poor baby."

He went away.

I scanned the action at the root beer stand while I waited for her to pick up. One scene involved a lover boy trying to steal the attention of a girl who was talking to a kid who looked even more insecure than I had at his age. To the tutored eye insecurity is as obvious as deformity. The other was a cute little girl sitting on the back bumper of a pickup truck sobbing into a handkerchief while all around her girls laughed and talked. Some real friends she had there.

No hello. "I'll be there for a month. Or so they tell me."

"I'm glad you're going."

"Of course you are. I won't be there to make sure you earn your paycheck."

"Oh, yeah, that's why you hired me. Because I'm so lazy."

A hesitation. "There're an awful lot of people who'll get a good chuckle out of me going to a hospital for drunks."

"To hell with them. You're doing what you need to do."

"I hope you're not expecting any corny speeches from me about how I've finally realized that I need help. I'll save all that for AA."

This time the hesitation was mine. "I hate to say this, but I'm going to miss you and I'm going to be praying for you."

"Now you're the one getting corny."

"I figured you'd say that."

"I want to be nice and sober when my friend Dick Nixon visits me here in July. And I don't want any remarks about Dick. He's my good friend and one of these days he's going to be president again." Then: "I'm scared, McCain."

"I know you are. But you'll make it. You're too strong not to."

"You really believe that?"

"I do, Your Honor. I do."

Hesitation. "They're going to make fun of me."

"And you'll make fun of them right back."

Hesitation. "You know that I like you more than I let on sometimes."

"You'd almost have to."

She laughed. "Yes, I would at that, wouldn't I?" Pause. "Now I'm the one in danger of being corny. Good-bye, McCain."

"Good-bye, Judge."

I doubted that she had tears in her eyes, but I sure did.

AT HOME I stripped to boxers, fixed an egg-and-ketchup sandwich, and sat on the couch watching the news.

The cats collected around me, ready for a good long sleep with, by default, their favorite human being.

Something Stan had said still bothered me, but not until now did I understand why. How had Marie Denham known that Will Neville had violated his probation?

I quickly called Stan. It took him a few minutes to

find the name of the school administrator he'd talked to the other day while following up on the David Leeds story. He didn't have the phone number. I had to call information for the home phone number of the guy.

Deep, aggrieved sigh. "Yes, this is he."

"I'm sorry to be calling so late, Mr. Tooker."

"Then why are you? This is a school night."

"This concerns Marie Denham."

"Who?"

"Marie Denham. A teacher at your school."

"I don't know who you are, but I've been principal here for eleven years and I've never heard of any Marie Denham."

We spent four or five minutes longer on the phone. He gave me no more useful information.

I next called the local hospital and got a report on Will Neville. He was listed in fair condition but was in the hospital overnight for observation. I asked if there was a phone in his room.

"Yes, there is, but you can't call him now."

I said, "May I have your name? I'm McClintock on the hospital board. In fact, my law firm takes care of all your legal matters."

I hated this particular game. Lying to an employee who could get in trouble if she let me have my way.

"I'll ring the number, sir."

When he picked up, he said, "I didn't even notice the phone when they rolled me in here. Who is this?"

"McCain."

"You son of a bitch."

"There isn't time for that now. You can call me all the names you want after this is settled."

"After what is settled? What are you talking about? Ouch. My damned head. You made it worse, you son of a bitch."

"What I'm talking about is you not being considered a suspect in these murders."

"I wouldn't kill my brother. Even the cops would know that."

"We're talking Cliffie here, remember? He might decide to come after you for those killings. You know Cliffie."

"What do you want?"

"I want to know who you and your brothers have been hiding from."

"This colored bitch—we were shaking down her father, or tryin' to. And he killed himself over it. She's been stalking us ever since."

Then he told me all about it, her real name and what she'd been up to. Now the murders made sense.

TWENTY-NINE

I PARKED IN A No Parking zone and rushed into the Greyhound terminal. The man behind the ticket counter looked shocked when he saw me running toward him.

Out of breath, I told him who I was looking for.

"That bus is leaving in about five minutes. She's probably already on it."

The loading area held only one bus. Most of the windows had passengers looking out them. At me.

The door was open. I climbed aboard. At first I couldn't see much. But after my eyes adjusted, it was easy enough to spot her. She sat in an aisle seat about halfway back. She sat with her head back. Her eyes seemed to be closed.

It was a busload of corpses for the most part, long-distance travelers so fatigued they slept through most stops.

I walked back to her, passing through sections of perfume, tobacco, unclean flesh, whiskey.

I couldn't tell if she was seeing me or not. Maybe she really was dozing.

"Hi, Marie."

The eyelids parted instantly. "I figured my luck would run out."

The woman next to her said, "Is everything all right?"

Marie said, "I killed some people. He's going to take me in."

"I need your wrist, Marie."

I handcuffed her to me and then we left the bus. Whispers hissed behind us.

A killer. Handcuffs. My God. A dull trip suddenly became an exciting one.

When we reached the pavement again, she said, "How about we get a tenderloin and some fries?"

"I won't let you get away."

"You want to hear about it or not, McCain?"

"And the price of hearing about it is—"

"A tenderloin and fries. And a Coke. Be a long, long time before I ever have food like that again."

THE BUS DEPOT DINER hadn't been redecorated in years.

The place was a time trip. Framed newspaper pages of World War II vintage; framed photographs of Joe Louis and Harry Truman and of course FDR; the most recent movie stars were Clark Gable and Ava Gardner. There was a museum feel to it all.

I'd taken the cuffs off outside. We sat at a wobbly Formica-covered table. An exhausted waitress dragged herself over and took our order.

"You had us all fooled, Diane."

"Diane?"

"You've used two other names since you got to town here. I don't blame you for being confused."

She just watched me. She knew it was over. Her dark and lovely eyes sparkled with tears.

"Diane Foster. The daughter of a Chicago alderman, the Reverend Thomas Foster. He was admired by black people and white people alike. Unique in Chicago politics in that he never took a bribe, never used his position to improve his own finances."

"Don't tell me about my father. He was the most wonderful man who ever lived."

"But he fell in love with a woman in church and they had an affair. She had a baby out of wedlock."

She angrily tapped a cigarette from her pack and put it in her mouth. I held my lighter out for her. She slapped it away.

"You keep your filthy thoughts about my father to yourself. You don't have the right to even speak his name."

"I'm not judging him. I'm explaining why you're here and why you murdered three people."

"Two people I murdered. Richie Neville and James Neville. David Leeds lunged at me after I shot that bastard Richie. I didn't mean to kill him at all. It was completely accidental."

"The woman your father had the affair with, she worked in the same office James Neville did. That's how those three found out about your father. They were already blackmailing several other people, so they just added him to the list."

She put her hand to her forehead. Tears gleamed on her cheeks now. "He didn't have any money. He just had his salary from the city council. He never even took a stipend from the church. He had to clean out all his savings to keep paying them. And then when he couldn't get any more money—"

I reached over and touched her hand. She jerked it away.

"You know the rest, McCain. He killed himself."

"And then you went looking for the Nevilles. One time you set their house on fire in the middle of the night but they got out all right. And two different times you shot at them. But they got away from that, too. They couldn't go to the police because they were blackmailers. And you didn't want to go to the police. You wanted your own vengeance."

She took the napkin from her side of the table and dabbed it against her eyes. "I didn't get Will. That's my only regret." She was composed again. She scanned my face. "I'm glad it's over."

"How'd you find them here in Black River Falls?"

"I hired a private investigator to find them. He tracked them to Black River Falls. I came here to kill them. I found Richie first. Unfortunately, David Leeds tried to stop me and I accidentally killed him. But then I realized if I was going to stay here I needed a reason so people wouldn't get suspicious—a Negro woman in this town sticks out—so I pretended to be David's sister. There was plenty of information about him on the news the next morning here and from Chicago, so it wasn't hard to fake."

"I'm sorry about your father."

"You didn't even know him."

"I'm sure he was every bit the man you said he was."

"Don't patronize me. That's the worst thing of all."

"I want to get you a lawyer."

A cold smile. "You don't want to represent me yourself?"

"I want to get you a better lawyer than I am. I haven't had any experience in murder trials."

"You let me worry about my lawyer. I don't need anything from you. Or from anybody."

"Is there anybody you want me to call?"

Her eyes shone again with tears. "I never thought of it before. I'm going to spend the rest of my life in Iowa. In prison. In Iowa." She touched a slender ebony finger to her cheek. "I was the one everybody thought would be such a success. Just wait till this gets on the news."

"For what it's worth, I'm sorry, Diane."

She smiled. "If 'sorrys' were worth anything, McCain, I'd be a rich woman."

THIRTY

SHE SAT AT THE COUNTER sipping coffee and smoking a cigarette, an air of isolation about her that old Edward Hopper would have appreciated. It had begun to drizzle, big hot drops dancing on the pavement, but the dampness felt good on my skin and so I stood across the street from the diner just watching her. She was a Sinatra song from just before the war, "Haunted Heart" or "Saturday Night Is the Loneliest Night of the Week" maybe, that sort of sad urban dignity right here in our little town of Black River Falls.

Except for the night man and Jane, the place was empty now. She raised her cup and he filled it for her. Then he went back to scraping the grill.

The rain started abruptly, as if some cosmic hand had flipped a switch. She turned at the sound of rumbling thunder. And saw me. She didn't acknowledge me in any way, not even a tiny tip of the head.

Then she was grabbing her umbrella and her brief-case and dropping a dollar bill on the countertop and walking toward the door.

Standing beneath the overhang of the place, she opened her umbrella and then came walking toward me across the empty street.

She didn't say anything even when she reached me,

just tugged me close beneath the shelter of her umbrella. I was gallant enough to relieve her of her briefcase.

We were getting wet, of course, because now the rain was such that not even a dozen umbrellas could keep feet and legs dry. Sewers ran with water; rivers formed at intersections.

But I didn't mind the rain at all. I was pretty sure I was going to get a real good kiss for all this trouble.